ACCLAIM

"It is refreshing to open the pages of a book written by a woman who died 23 years ago without publishing. At the time, her book was considered too tawdry for publication.

Her book tells the universal tale of the rise and fall of a community, its complicated inhabitants, told in a bold, amusing, and absorbing narrative. It tells the historical tale of the effects building a dam has on this small community, living in a remote part of a state.

Ms. North weaves her story around memorable characters like Maggie Tiffany, and the Trooper Jim Hadden, adept at serving the law, as well as satisfying his own laws of nature."

Yvette Nachmias-Beau, author, *Ledicia's Key, A Reluctant Life, Best Friends, Clara at Sixy*

"Written over 60 years ago, In the Shadow of the Dam, is a gem of a novel. Reminiscent of Peyton Place, we are introduced to the small town of Gainesville, New York in the post WWII era. With vivid description and entertaining dialogue, the author skillfully brings each character to life. We come to know both the sinners and the saints and will not soon forget them or the events that shaped their lives."

Theresa Schimmel, author, *Yankee Girl in Dixie, David's War/Davide's Peace, Sunny,, Braided Secrets* and others

"The very fact that North's book is finally published is an example of giving thanks to the special individuals each of us has had in our lives, gentle mentors who helped us discover our passions and come to a better place."

I. Michael Grossman, author, *Shrinkwrapped; The Accidental President, The Realm* and others

"A charmingly candid book that speaks of a time when 'unspeakable things' were kept quiet- with unpredictable results. A great read and lovely homage to a time, a town – and a woman – that should not be forgotten."

Kim Hansen, essays, *Fast Fallen Women, Fast Famous Women*

"Bertha "Van" Edwards North, my grandmother, was no stranger to tragedy and heartbreak. She encountered many hardships in life including the death of two children in infancy, and she struggled to raise four daughters on her own in the wake of the sudden death of her husband in 1949. In her characteristic style, she braved adversity, shrugged off the pain and kept moving forward. There is no doubt in my mind that the challenges she faced strengthened her resolve, reshaping her life, emphasizing adaptation and strength over helplessness and victimhood. It is not surprising that the unfortunate circumstances impacted her writing as well.

Bertha became a nurse, a profession that highlighted her selfless nature. I remember her as a strong, confident presence with an uncommon reserve of empathy. My grandmother instilled in me, aside from a love of literature and writing, a sense of wonder and creativity that can only be shared among kindred spirits. Like my grandmother, the challenges I faced in life surfaced in my writing. I can relate to her in that coping with challenges in life through writing is as cathartic as it gets."

David Annese, author, *Chasing the Sun, The Blue Rails of Time*

IN THE SHADOW
OF THE DAM

BERTHA 'VAN'
EDWARDS NORTH
with Bill Seymour

Publisher's Information

©Bill Seymour, 2025

ISBN 978-1-953080-59-2

Author contact:
Billwriter629@gmail.com

EBookBakery Books

Purpose, Passion and Proffer
By Bill Seymour

 Bertha "Van" Edwards North, a nurse for most of her adult life, wrote this book more than 60 years ago. The manuscript was rejected by publishers at the time and it was dismissed in the mid-1960s as too tawdry. But today, its unvarnished truth resonates and is acceptable, even tame by today's standards. Its fiction reveals lives rarely spoken of—quiet, complex, and real—and their fates. My grandmother died 23 years before I started editing this unpublished work of hers. In many ways, this book is a bridge back to her voice. Both the beginning and the end, the first and the last. While fictional, it is also semi-autobiographical.

It is now time to publish it with a proper dedication to her children, Gloria, George, Jeanne, Linda, Camilla and Terri, to her many grandchildren, to her mother, Rosa Lee M. Edwards, her father, William H. Edwards, and her stepfather, McKinley Edwards, and all her brothers and sisters who so influenced her life. Those people in Downsville, N.Y., now long dead, but with shadows of themselves in this book, deserve a nod from my grandmother.

Also, to Holly, Kathleen, Will, Meg and their children, Grace and Mara. Friends like the late Melody Currey, Rev. Robert F. Tucker, Nikki Munroe and Tony Sciolto who helped me in immeasureable ways, too.

And to Dr. Barry Lewis for helping me discover the emotional resilience, coupled with insight, to reconcile the loss of my grandmother and to make editing of this book possible; to Drs. Steven R. Fera, C. Steven Wolf, Rob P. Weinstein, Michael B. Fischer, William H. Ramsey and Brendan Campbell, along with Garry Lapidus, PA-C for their candor, friendship and sensitivity, so much a part of the medical profession my grandmother prized.

So we beat on, boats against the current, borne back ceaselessly into the past.

–**F. Scott Fitzgerald,** *The Great Gatsby* (1925)

CHAPTERS

Prologue

This historical-fiction novel is set in Gainsville, a pseudonym for Downsville, a village in the Town of Colchester, N.Y., and in the state's Catskill region. Between 1947 and 1954, the Pepacton Reservoir on the East Branch in Delaware County was built to feed the voracious New York City water supply system, which was created in the early nineteen hundreds.

These days, some hard times have settled over this tiny village—so different now from the place Bertha "Van" Edwards North once lovingly called "up home," an area where she spent the early years of her life and where she frequently visited. More than 60 years have passed since she wrote *In The Shadow of The Dam*, capturing the bittersweet spirit of a town caught between memory and progress. She never lived to witness its slow unraveling. To her, Downsville and nearby Corbett formed a quilt of rustic comforts and quiet heartbreak—a rural cradle of youth, stitched with longing and pride. But life pulled her toward Middletown, N.Y., a distant city pulsing with promises that her hometown area could never offer. What was left behind was not forgotten, only frozen in time.

Middletown and Downsville may lie within the same region of the state, but the road between them tells a story of distance—geographic and cultural. Stretching some 70 miles across winding mountain roads, the drive from Middletown to Downsville today takes roughly 90 minutes, but can feel more tedius as the urban bustle gives way to deep woods and disappearing cell service. In the 1940s the trip took longer without the current highway system.

The most traveled route rolls west along NY-17 to Roscoe—known as Trout Town, USA—before veering north on NY-206, where signs grow sparse and the landscape rises into the folds of the Catskills. An alternate path diverts through Liberty and across back roads that trace the shadows of forgotten rail lines and rivers dammed decades ago.

Either way, the journey underscores just how far you have to go to reach a place like Downsville—a hamlet tucked behind the walls of the Pepacton Reservoir, hidden in plain sight.

It is nestled within the western Catskill Mountains, a rugged and forested region in southeastern New York State.

Campbell Mountain is just east of Downsville and rises to about 2,800 feet with scenic views over the Pepacton Reservoir. Bryden Mountain rises to the southwest with punishing rugged terrain surrounding the hamlet.

Northwest of Downsville is Mary Smith Hill, while south of the reservoir and a part of the southwestern Catskills is Brock Mountain and northwest is the hiking, horseback riding and camping backcountry and trailhead Bear Spring Mountain.

While not surrounded by towering peaks, it is enveloped by this network of lower-elevation mountains and ridges characteristic of the Catskill Plateau.

The city of New York designed its Catskill water network in 1905 and the Catskill Aqueduct System was finished by 1924. By 1931, the city had won the blessing of the U.S. Supreme Court to expand its upstate infrastructure. It was accepted that rural towns that stood in the way of the city's water supply would be submerged. Pepacton, Union Grove, Shavertown and Arena were the four hamlets that resided in a valley slated to be transformed into the Pepacton Reservoir, and the Downsville Dam, both the largest ever built by the city.

A history of the actual dam construction and surrounding changes to the landscape of the area was painted by Professor Lucy Sante in her book, *Nineteen Reservoirs - On Their Creation and the Promise of Water for New York City*, with illustrator Tim Davis (2022, *The Experiment* publisher). As Sante and *The New York Review of Books* wrote in a review of her book: From 1907 to 1967, a network of reservoirs and aqueducts was built across more than one million acres in upstate New York, including Greene, Delaware, Sullivan, and Ulster Counties.

This feat of engineering served to meet New York City's ever-increasing need for water, sustaining its inhabitants and cementing it as a center of industry. West of the Hudson, it meant that many villages, with their farms, forest lands, orchards, and quarries, were bought for a fraction of their value, demolished, and submerged, profoundly altering ecosystems in ways we will never fully appreciate for the overall water system network.

An influx of over 65 engineers from the Board of Water Supply of New York City moved to the village. More than 13,000 acres of land was taken and five small adjacent communities were lost to create this reservoir.

The reservoir project brought in over 350 workers and their families. Many local residents and veterans returning from World War II went to work on the reservoir project attracted by the union wages of between $2 to $2.25 per hour. Downsville was a Boom Town.

The Board of Water Supply was responsible for planning and overseeing the construction of reservoirs and aqueducts to ensure a steady supply of clean drinking water for the city. The BWS was also responsible for moving cemeteries in the reservoir area. In the Town of Colchester, they moved 183 graves from the Edget, 33 from the Cat Hollow, 26 from the Shaver, 11 from the Flynn and one from the Sickler cemeteries.

After the completion of the Pepacton Reservoir, *The Walton Reporter* on February 4, 1955, posed this question:

"The one big question in the minds of the long-time residents is what will happen to Downsville when the workers, engineers and families move on to their next project. Will it be a 'Ghost Town'? It is my guess that because of the territory, and the large body of scenic beauty of the surrounding water, Downsville will become a summer resort. Motels and summer cottages will spring up and the trade from tourists and vacation seekers will keep the little community alive."

That prophecy has come to pass. One of Downsville's major sources of income has been from tourism, seasonal homes in "the country" as New York City dwellers call upstate New York and service to others who visit and pass through the community, town officials say in a history of the dam project. In addition, more than two-thirds of its tax levy is paid by a single property owner, the City of New York.

Bertha "Van" Edwards North had a childhood and continued connection to that area as the dam was built. Through the fictional characters and scenes in her novel, she captures how this changed forever the real lives of people living in Downsville and their futures for good and ill. She also offered a semi-autobiographical portrait of herself as Becky.

In The Shadow of the Dam opens with life before the dam became a center point for community change.

Firestorms, Whiskey and Secrets

The small town rested on the valley's rim. Verdant mountains shaded it when the sun was high, casting elusive shadows draped intermittently in intricate patterns of golden sunlight. Silver-crested brooks mothered by perpetual springs rippled merrily down the mountainside. Mischievously splashing against the rocks and leaping in the air, they somersaulted on to join their destiny—the East Branch of the Delaware River that flowed through the valley.

It was virgin territory, unfettered and unhampered in the 1940s and in the decades and centuries beforehand. Its population of nearly 600 had grown slowly over time to nearly 1,000 people. However, as younger men were called to serve in World War II, Gainesville, New York, was beginning to see a decline in its economy.

Forests had been stripped, and lumbering and tanneries were going out of business, and the Depression slowed construction in the cities, suppressing stone and lumber markets. Prices were low on farm produce, and farmers were struggling to make the land pay.

The people inhabiting the town were content. They seldom left the valley, having little need. Self-sufficiency abounded, but only a few profited materially from it. Their knowledge of other ways of living could have been improved, perhaps enhancing their satisfaction. The young grew up and assumed their place in community life as a natural sequence when the old passed. It sounds peaceful. It was.

Its underside packed the potential of a sleeping volcano whose rumbles came every so often, and time could not stop the lava from eventually flowing out.

Main Street, named so for obvious reasons, ran the entire town from north to south. Here and there, a side street came in to meet it and backed away to the town's eastern or western limits. Tree-shaded lawns bordered these streets where most of the town's inhabitants lived.

The Gainesville combined elementary and high school, taking its name from the town, imposed its lofty mien upon the inhabitants as its teachers tried to teach high standards to those caught in poverty and sagging ambition. Located at the end of Main Street, it also served as Gainesville's northern boundary.

At the terminus of Main to the south, a nondescript firehouse, more aptly termed "The Shed," housed the old fire truck and defined the town's southern line. The very few business enterprises the town supported were scattered between these two longitudinal points.

Someone from a city might see the town as picturesque in a quaint fashion. Undoubtedly, there would be delight at the unexpected rustic sight of the roughly built plank bridge on Main Street spanning Elder Brook that flowed across town on its course to join the Delaware River, visible from the town's southern point.

The brook kept a constant melodious tone flowing as a mother cradled a suckling babe to her breast, softly humming a tune that had never materialized in song or been set to music. A timeless, ageless sound stilled for a moment in a limbo of forgetfulness, then was heard again in lapping shore waters of the sea or in the soft soughing of the pines.

Five or six feet from the northern end of the plank bridge, set close to the sidewalk, was a small building owned by Giuseppe Vignola, one of the town's two barbers. He used the building's first floor for his barber shop, or "tonsorial parlor," as he chose to call it. Maggie Tiffany rented the living quarters upstairs. She could lean from her window and spit into the water that ran near the building.

Maggie liked the sound of its gurgling splash, and it was pleasant to gaze upon, except when it was really shallow, exposing its litter-strewn bottom.

At these times, debris clearly showed. James Borton, the town doctor, deemed it a menace to public health and advised the town to have it covered over. Nothing had been achieved in the way of a solution. The Town Council decided unanimously that Doc's findings were inconclusive and that it would be preposterous to dip into the town's meager funds for such a project.

So the brook flowed on undisturbed, sometimes swelling its banks in the season of heavy rains, other times barely covering the rubbish. Because of that sight—maybe even a health hazard—Maggie rented her apartment for a few dollars a month from Giuseppe but seldom laid out cash.

Giuseppe, squat and swarthy, reeked of barbering tonics and lacked a wife. He was on the shady side of 40 years old and propitiously inclined toward Maggie. However, he maintained a discreet residence at the local Eagle Hotel.

The hotel, separated from the firehouse by a half dozen houses, was owned and managed by a widowed mother and son. It kept a respectable front by boarding the two state troopers designated to maintain law and order in the valley.

The town closed its ears to the rumor that the younger of these two was lascivious when the occasion arose. No word yet had spread about a recent occasion next door to the hotel. Polly Howe lived there with her mother. Just over 17 years old, she knew little of artificial laws or those of nature.

Trooper Jim Hadden, a few years younger than his partner, was adept at serving the law of the land and satisfying the law of nature within himself, keeping the one separate from the other when possible. Infringement seldom occurred, but in the case of Polly, it had. He was quite the man in and out of uniform.

He proved it by teaching Polly the rudiments of her voluptuous body. It was simple. He acquainted himself with Mrs. Howe's evening schedule. He knew exactly when she would be absent.

He could set his watch by her comings and goings. As soon as her mother left, Polly would start her shenanigans. He would watch her as she moved seductively back and forth in front of her bedroom window in her ultra-sheer nightgown. It enticed his ever-developing interest. A few flirtatious smiles and small but meaningful conversations finally culminated in his walking across the side lawn one moonless night, rapping softly on her window and heisting himself over the sill when she opened it.

Running his hands over her soft curves, they were easy to remember. He would eventually have to resort to that little "Merry Widows" box in his pocket. Still, he couldn't see himself fathering a mountain brat born of a few hours' diversion.

Then, too, ever-present in his mind lingered the thought of his captain's daughter. She didn't appeal to his physical senses, but she had made it quite evident that she more than liked him and just as apparent that marriage to her would influence his ranking and supervising headquarters captain—some distance away from this hamlet—to promote him in his present career.

He tossed that distracting thought aside.

Trooper Jim had whetted his appetite too long, and after getting this far with Polly, he wasn't about to stop now. His visits became regular and less enthusiastic after a few weeks.

Jim's partner, Trooper Bill Sloan, knew of this nocturnal romance but slept soundly through his absence. The troopers lived at the hotel to provide what little police protection was needed. Sloan could escape a nagging wife for five days of the week.

Sound sleep also helped Sloan turn a blind eye to the hum of a motor from a car as it pulled out from the back of the hotel loaded with bootleg whiskey. What the hell? No one could prove he knew about it.

He had never witnessed it and therefore couldn't swear to it. He liked living at the hotel. The food was good, and his room was comfortable. The twenty bucks he found under his bureau scarf every Monday morning had nothing to do with it.

Just because the hotel owner's son drove a Marquette coupe with a similar-sounding motor didn't mean a damn thing, either. All things reckoned, he and Jim had many reasons for liking to live at the hotel.

Across from the hotel, the Tomlin store crowded the flagstone sidewalk. An aged sign, suspended on rusty chains from the entrance overhang, identified the type of merchandise to be found within. With its disorganized array of wares, the store was as old and musty-smelling as old man Stan Tomlin, its owner. He made a bare living, and that was all. He held a redoubtable position in town, which was sufficient for Mr. Tomlin.

Traveling north on the same side of the street, opposite Jake's restaurant and the A&P store, stood the only fireproof building the town could boast. Constructed of concrete blocks and three stories high, it gave Main Street its only impressive feature. It was called the Shaw building, named after its first owner long ago, now worm-eaten in the old cemetery at the edge of town.

At street level, the building's main floor was divided equally by a long and vast hall terminating in a double stairway spiraling upward to the spacious second floor where the Saturday night picture show could be seen for a 25-cent admission fee. Granted, the films weren't the latest Hollywood productions by the time they were projected on the Gainesville screen, but few knew the difference or would have cared if they had.

It was an escape from the everyday tensions of complex, often unrewarding work. For a couple of hours, they sat there watching. They were transported to another world.

Two bits couldn't possibly buy them greater pleasure elsewhere. After the show closed, some of the daring younger group, seeking an added thrill, left by the fire escape exits on either side of the building. It was forbidden, but the manager needed help to enforce the rule. Most of the patrons, however, descended the spiraling stairway to the floor below.

Half of this floor, to the right of the hall as one faced it from the street, comprised the one-room drugstore. It was stocked with a fair assortment of drugs, cosmetic sundries, and the only soda fountain in town. Venerable Mr. John Wilson, the druggist, moved about his counters leisurely, exchanging pleasantries with his customers now and then, casting a sly appreciative eye over the better points of his female customers. Evaluated by the town's standards, his was a lucrative business.

To the left of the drugstore, the town's bank occupied the other half of the main floor. Here, dignity and respect were symbolized in the expansive carpeted room with its offices firmly ensconced behind the steel mesh enclosure. The large plate glass window fronting Main Street boldly flaunted the inscription, "First National Bank."

It was held in esteem mainly because it represented money, and the people around had so damn little of it.

People moved unhurriedly along the streets of Gainesville with an aura of unparalleled contentment. A birth or death in the village was an event showing keen interest—congratulations or condolences or sometimes both, depending on the person. Either or both happened immediately as the rumor mill cranked out the news.

It was, after all, a country town. The only thing spreading faster was a brush fire in the dry woods during a hot summer.

There wasn't much excitement usually. However, it was occasionally aroused when a fire would break out, sometimes in the town, but more often in the surrounding forests. The small and ancient fire truck, manned by a volunteer crew of the village, would hustle to the scene. It finally ended its career of usefulness in the epic effort the town firefighters made to help quell the forest fire on Campbell Mountain.

It was rumored the fire had been set deliberately by Eli Campbell, one of the old mountaineers residing in that neck of the woods. He and the other mountain dwellers had chopped and corded wood from boyhood to earn a living, eventually clearing enough of the land to build cabin homes for their families. That summer, they learned the state would claim the land for reforestation. Land that they had only squatters' rights to begin with. The woodchoppers, barely earning enough to subsist on, muttered angrily.

The 1929 State Reforestation Act and the 1931 Hewitt Amendment authorized the New York State Conservation Department to acquire land outside the Forest Preserve to be used for reforestation.

These State Reforestation Areas, consisting of not less than 500 acres of contiguous land, were to be "forever devoted to reforestation and the establishment and maintenance thereon of forests for watershed protection, the production of timber, and for recreation and kindred purposes."

A majority were abandoned farmland with depleted soils and significant erosion issues. The Conservation Department wanted to begin a massive tree-planting program to restore these lands for watershed protection, flood prevention, and future timber production.

Old man Campbell muttered the loudest. Known throughout the mountains for his indomitable courage and nonconformity to anything alien to his feudal nature, Eli Campbell may have avenged the state by setting the fire, but no one could prove it. The mountain people clammed up when outsiders questioned them. They all knew who it was shortly after Eli's journey through that neck of the woods where the fire broke out.

The flames hid in the thick underbrush for days before roaring up the tall trees. It was a raging inferno. Gainesville threw down its everyday routine to battle this hell of Satan. The fire truck, manned by the village volunteer crew, raced to the scene, followed by a few stragglers, some women, a few hours later. The fire truck backed up to a small brook and drenched the fire as far as its hose could throw the water.

A human water line, assembled of men and boys, passed buckets of water from hand to hand to the fire's edge in an ineffectual attempt to quench the blaze. Women lugged jugs of coffee as near to the men as deemed safe. Thick sandwiches of homemade bread and smoked ham were piled high on a vast, flat rock that served as an improvised table. The women were of no small help, aiding wherever they could. Occasionally, a husky one replaced a man in the water brigade while he ate or drank.

The fire gained momentum, and men from all over the valley answered an appeal for more help. The mountain swarmed with them. The fire cast shadows of them wielding picks and shovels, hastily digging a trench, then starting a fire beyond it to run and meet its adversary. For four days and three nights, the central fire hopped from tree to tree until finally, at the edge of the trench, it sank in defeat to the ground.

The acrid odor of smoke hung over the valley for days. That smell and the charred, barren wastes for miles around were the only reminders of an imminent threat of destruction.

While this vast desolate barrenness was still exposed, and Gainesville, with its neighboring farms, was still shaken by its proximity to complete disaster, the volunteer fire company immediately presented its formerly ignored plea for a new fire engine to town officials.

Marvin Dulle, the bank president, also filled Gainesville's mayoral position. He had favored the fire department's request on three previous occasions it had been brought to his attention, but the town council had vetoed it each time. Given the latest fire and the fire department's present request, he decided now was the strategic time to exercise his right to call the council members together in an emergency.

One evening, the members met with the Mayor as requested. The meeting was called to order. Mayor Dulle rose from his chair.

"We'll dispose of formalities, gentlemen. I'm sure you know why we're assembled here." His voice suddenly reached thunderous tones. "We're going to do now that which we should have done four years ago when the fire department made its first request for a dependable, adequate fire truck. We're going to grant that request here and now, that is," he emphasized.

"If you're conscientious and responsible enough to be members of this council. We're not only going to vote for just a better truck, we're going to vote for a new one. The town will have to go into debt to pay for it, but without adequate fire equipment, one of these days there'll be no town," he said.

"We'll either consent to negotiate for a new truck at this meeting, or I'll take it up independently with the town proper for popular consideration. Of course, you're fully aware, or should be, that a thumbs-down decision this evening won't help you any at next election time, either," the mayor warned.

Homer Gladrock, one of the more aggressive councilmen, rose to his feet. "Suppose you tell us, Mr. Mayor, how this town can purchase a $16,000 fire truck with only $1,500 or less in the town's till." Rapping his knuckles nervously against the back of the chair before him, he continued talking.

"Why can't we have the present truck overhauled? The cost would be nominal, and we wouldn't have a breath-squeezing debt hanging over our heads. However, the most pressing question is this: How would we get that much money? Just like that?" He snapped his fingers disparagingly.

"Now, at last, we're getting to pertinent matters," the Mayor replied, unperturbed. He picked up a sheaf of papers from the table beside him. "Here," he said, slapping the papers back and forth on his hand.

"Here's the answer. I had these papers drawn up this afternoon. They're the sum and total of an application for a long-term loan from the bank to the town of Gainesville. It only requires your signatures. As president of the bank, I can assure you it will be approved and handled with the utmost expediency."

He laid the papers back on the table. "Now, gentlemen, shall we take a vote and get this business over with?"

"Business it is," Homer Gladrock murmured to the councilman beside him. "Mainly business for the bank with six percent interest tacked to the loan. Just watch out, taxes hike now."

"Does anyone have anything further to say before we vote?" The Mayor directed his question to the entire group, but his cold, penetrating gaze seemed to rest longer on Homer Gladrock. Homer suddenly remembered his pending application for a personal loan from the bank and pursed his lips silently.

"We're ready, Mr. Mayor," announced Homer, finance subcommittee chairman, as he passed out slips of paper to the group and took a seat.

A few minutes of silence followed. The chairman rose, collected the papers he had passed out, and handed them to the Mayor. He accepted them enthusiastically and proceeded to read the voting results. He rubbed his hands together approvingly.

"I'm certainly pleased that you men approved this measure. It not only shows you are worthy of the town's trust but of the bank's as well." His smile beamed over them like a beacon light. Homer eased his tense position in his chair.

When Gainesville later received its new fire engine, the firefighters displayed it regally by organizing the largest parade ever to march through the streets of Gainesville. They set a date and invited the firefighting units in the rest of the valley to join them.

Such an invitation was unprecedented in the small valley.

Each town held its parade on Memorial Day, and the firefighters were an integral part of it, but no town in the valley had ever invited the firefighters to mass in one colossal parade. It was a novel idea, and the valley residents greeted it with enthusiasm.

At the Mayor's suggestion, Gainesville made plans for a barbecue to be held after the parade, with the proceeds to be applied to the town's indebtedness. It seemed the Mayor's popularity zoomed overnight. The town had a strong propensity to lionize someone at one time or another, and this time, they chose the Mayor. They conceded he was a man of brilliance in any capacity he decided to fill and acclaimed him long and loudly.

Dulle enjoyed both his public reputation and his acumen in business. It was like looking at himself in a mirror and getting two different reflections of the same man. As a final gesture of kindness and goodwill toward the town, and with an eye toward next year's election, he donated a fair portion of his salary as Mayor back to the town's coffers.

Gainesville was up and about its business bright and early on the parade day. The weather turned crisp and refreshing. By ten o'clock, a heterogeneous crowd moved through the streets.

An hour later, as scheduled, the parade formed on the high school grounds, wound its way down a side street, up Maple at the east end of town, turned at its junction with Main, and proceeded through the business section. By marching slowly and pausing often, the firemen managed to keep the parade on the streets for two hours, finally disbanding in the field at the rear of the opera house or Shaw building. The barbecue was ready and waiting, with a delicious aroma of roasted beef permeating the air.

The new fire engine, red as the blood of the men who operated it, was parked near the edge of the field, circled by a group of men. Old Johnny Garrett limped or staggered—no one watching could determine which it was—to the side of the engine. Precariously holding his balance, he mounted the steps of the machine.

"Here, this will make a fire your old engine can't put out," he joked, handing over an earthen jug to the fireman sitting at the wheel. The driver lifted the jug to his mouth with a crook of his elbow, swallowed a mouthful of its fiery contents, and passed it along to the next fireman. "Tain't nothin' but Adam's ale," Johnny innocently told the bystanders.

The town's two state troopers, standing at the fringe of the crowd, turned and walked quickly over to the barbecue pit. Johnny retrieved his jug, doffed his old sweat-stained felt hat that he wore year-round, and laughed uproariously. Finally, the men dispersed around the fire truck to find seats at the rapidly filling tables. There was chaos of noise and good-natured banter as they started eating.

Maggie Tiffany, a long-time colorful resident of Gainesville, sat at one of the smaller tables with her special cronies. Johnny Garrett wedged his bulk in between her and Jenny Hilbur.

"Best damn feed this town ever put on, eh, Maggie?" he grinned as he crammed his mouth full.

"Can't say as I enjoy some of the company too good, Johnny, but this here is mighty tasty beef all the same. Guess I'll have some more. How about you, Jennie?"

The two rose from the table and carried their plates back to the barbecue pit. Grace Hill, who had been serving the patrons, saw them coming and suddenly became busy, deliberately keeping her back to them. Jake, her husband supervising the barbecue, moved forward and put a large slice of meat on each of their plates, gave Jennie a sly wink, then turned to serve someone else.

The ladies who had been helping Grace serve pulled their skirts noticeably aside as Maggie and Jennie returned to their table. Grace cast an intense, long look at Jake's back and started serving again.

"It 'pears to me you did a right good business today, Johnny," Maggie said as she squeezed in beside him.

"Leastways, by the looks of Jake, I'd say so."

"Twarn't bad, Maggie, considering 'twas right under the noses of the law," Johnny said. His laugh resounded loudly amidst the crowd.

The two state troopers glanced Johnny's way momentarily, then shifted back to their eating. They ate with relish, partly due to the Mayor's benevolence. They appeared either too absorbed in eating or talking to notice that occasionally a jug was passed surreptitiously at some of the tables or to be aware of Johnny's frequent trips to his old truck with some of the firefighters. Immediately after eating, the two troopers returned to the hotel.

By late afternoon, only a few stragglers remained on the barbecue grounds. The women had cleared the tables and left except for Grace Hill.

"I'll wait for Jake," she had informed them when they had asked her to join them. She made her way to the edge of the field, where some firemen were preparing to depart on the fire truck. They had been joking with Jake, who was still laughing loudly.

"Come on, Jake, let's go," Grace said, laying her hand on his arm. "Nearly everyone else has left. Besides, you're two-thirds drunk now," she ended accusingly.

"I'm just going to take a little ride with the boys," Jake answered, immediately on the defensive. "You go on home, Grace. I'll be there shortly."

His drunken belligerence was a cue to the other men, and Jess Cable called out admiringly, "Atta boy, Jake," and held out his hand to aid Jake aboard the truck. With one short wail of its siren, Jess edged the truck slowly over the bumpy field and headed back toward town.

Someone in the back of Grace laughed mockingly. Grace recognized Maggie's raucous voice and clenched her fists tightly as Johnny Garrett limped past with Maggie and Jennie clinging to his arms.

Her face became red, and her body tensed with helpless rage as she gazed after them. She suspected from experience that before the night was ended, Jake and a good portion of the other men would be in bed with one or the other of them.

Abruptly, Grace turned on her heel and started walking in the opposite direction.

POLLY ARRIVES AS INNOCENCE DIES

Fall and winter in Gainesville were nothing to speak of. Residents did their deer hunting and hung the nailed animals by their feet near the general store before gutting them and preparing the venison for suppers in the months ahead.

Of course, this annual display was also part of a contest to see who captured the biggest one and which buck had the most points on its antlers, a kind of self-image for the men in Gainesville who measured girth and points only at the level just below the waist and directly between the legs.

The harsh winters of hibernation, drinking, and waiting for the season and snow to be over ebbed now into spring. The breeze had blown free from the icy fingers of winter. It teased and tossed the full skirts of Polly Howe and Leda Bard as they crossed the plank bridge on their way to high school. Polly giggled as Leda pulled at her skirt to keep it decorously below her knees. She didn't mind if her well-rounded thighs showed momentarily and suddenly deplored Leda's affected modesty.

"For heaven's sake, Leda, cut it out. You look something like a scarecrow or worse, holding your skirt down like that."

"Okay! If you want to show your ass, I will too," Leda laughed.

They paused at the end of the bridge and stood leaning over the rail, looking down at the gushing water.

"Aren't you thrilled to death to think we're going to graduate in just two more months?" Polly asked Leda.

"Umm," Leda replied, "but I'm not going to college, and you are, so you'll still be going to school. I'm glad I'm really finished studying. I always hated it."

"Yeah, I do too," Polly admitted, "but you know my mother. She believes in higher education, and that is that. She wants me to be a teacher simply because she's one. I can't see where she gets any fun out of teaching that bunch of little brats up in Cat Holler, but she must because that's all she's ever done except boss me around and Dad, too, when he was alive. I bet he was glad to be rid of her, even if he did have to die to do it."

"Polly Howe! That's an awful thing to say," Leda protested.

"Well, everyone says he drank himself to death, and I bet that's why," Polly said heatedly. "I know that is the only reason I'm going to college. I'm tired of her saying 'No' to everything I want to do. Do you remember the big argument I had with her before she finally let me have my own room downstairs?"

"She kept insisting," Polly continued, "that I wasn't old enough to sleep alone downstairs. She finally let me have my way because she thought I'd get sick from crying so hard. Can you imagine, Leda, just how silly it would seem if your mother sent you to bed every night at nine o'clock and then insisted on coming in and kissing you goodnight?"

"Well, I won't let her do it anymore. I lock my door and tell her I'm busy 'till she goes away. I like being kissed, but not by her," she added, with a wry smile.

"Oh, Polly, stop pouting," Leda said, "my mother says we're the two worst spoiled girls in town."

Suddenly, a gust of wind pasted Polly's blouse to her body, molding the sheer material over and around her breasts until they resembled ice cream cones thrusting out their pointed ends under her blouse.

"Polly, you look like one of those statues they have on radiator caps on the new cars," Leda giggled. Forgetting her gripes, Polly started laughing, thinking how she'd look on a radiator cap.

Startled out of their giggling by a sharp tinkle on glass, Polly and Leda glanced up at the rooms over the barbershop. Old Maggie waved to them through the dirty window and was promptly ignored. Mumbling something about a crazy old witch, the girls hurried to school.

Maggie grinned unperturbed, pulled her chair closer to the window, and raised it a few inches to let in the fresh air.

She often sat by that window, watching the people as they passed up and down the street. They often paused on the bridge to chat with a neighbor, admire a new baby, or, if a man spit a stream of golden tobacco juice into the brook below. Maggie harrumphed to herself as she recalled that spit wasn't the only thing ever mixed with that water.

She well remembered the night with Tom Shields, the town's half-assed electrician. There also was Jake Hill, who owned the restaurant down the street, and, of course, Guiseppe, the barber. All had gotten boozed up and knocked on her door at three o'clock in the morning.

Maggie had entertained them before, but only one at a time. This particular night, they were so drunk that Maggie figured they'd probably take an hour apiece, so she told the son-of-a-bitches to get the hell out. She watched as they stumbled down the stairs to the street and stopped under a light on the bridge.

She could see their shadowy figures plainly once her eyes adjusted to the darkness. Their voices were clear enough, too, coming through her open window. Over their drunken laughter, she heard Tom tell Jake to squirt it over the rail. Jake did, too, followed by Tom and Guiseppe. The top of the bridge rail was a six-inch plank, and by the time they quit fooling around, they had decided Jake had the longest. Maggie chuckled as she watched and finally called out her window to them.

"You bastards are purely right about Jake. Now go on home afore you wake up the whole town." The three men looked up at the window.

"You bitch, you, Maggie," Tom called to her. "Why did you make us waste all that goody?"

Maggie laughed, closed her window, and went to bed. The following morning, she had laughed when she found a ten-dollar bill shoved under her door. "I swear," she said aloud, "them damn fools have got more money than brains. I'd never open my head to nary a body 'bout 'em, but leastways they think their shenanigans won't be told of now."

The sudden slamming of the barbershop door downstairs brought Maggie out of her musings.

Swaying slightly in her chair, she lifted a brown earthen jug from the floor and tilted it to her lips. The corn squeezin' was solid and smooth, and Maggie swore it was the only thing that kept her breakfast down in the morning. She shook the jug after wiping her mouth on the back of her scurvy hand. "Not much left," she reflected, setting the jug down again. Staring off into space, she dozed off and on.

Once seemingly awake, she waggled her forefinger in a threatening gesture and started muttering aloud. "Johnny Garrett, you just better get in here this night with a jug of corn squeezin's, or you're gonna do your screwin' around with someone else."

Suddenly, her hand dropped, drawing an explosive curse from Maggie as it banged hard on the edge of a rocker's arm.

"Must a been dreamin',' 'twarnt Johnny in here at all," she said as she rubbed the side of her hand. She reached for the jug, swallowed a hooker, and laughed senselessly. Half-drunk, she started thinking about Johnny again, trying to recall whether it was last week or the week before when he visited her last. She couldn't remember, but she did know they had locked the door against intrusion and drunk enough corn liquor to float a raft of logs before they tumbled into bed together.

"Sometimes," she thought, "Johnny is good company, like he was that night." Other times she swore he didn't know his ass from a hole in the ground. That night, he had kept harking back to the days when they were just young'uns. He had reminded her of how she used to taunt the young bucks with her dreamy eyes and wriggly hips. She had gotten away with it, too, until the night she went out with Johnny. He had called off the sets at a square dance and asked to see her home when it ended.

Johnny always laughed like hell when he reminded Maggie of the rest of that night. On the way home, he 'whoa'd' his horse to a stop, lifted Maggie from the buggy, and carried her out to a cock of hay in the roadside field. Maggie didn't struggle; she hadn't wanted to. Johnny swore he couldn't rightly tell if he was raping Maggie or if she was raping him. Maggie loved it then, and she still did. For some reason, she never got "expecting."

Maybe there were too many men seeking and finding favor with her. Maggie held fast to the theory that what one man left there, the next one pushed out. That was if it wasn't too long in between. She had skipped the blessing of marriage, but knew all the calls of nature. She answered them fully, with one man after another.

Time had handled Maggie's face with reckless fingers, though it had done nothing to dull the charm she seemed to hold for the opposite sex.

Not quite 40 years old, with jet-black hair that was her secret joy, Maggie had managed to earn a vicarious living through the years. Occasionally, she'd give up her bed to Jenny Hilbur and one of her ever-changing admirers. With fewer years upon her than Maggie, Jenny plied her profession skillfully and remuneratively, sharing whatever needed to be shared with Maggie.

On the nights Jenny used the bedroom, Maggie dozed and chortled in drunken glee in the chair by the window. There was no doubt about it - Maggie was a survivor and swore through the gap in her rotten teeth she always would be.

The grinding of gears in the old yellow school bus as it stopped, then proceeded across the plank bridge to pick up its next riders, focused Maggie's bleary gaze out the window again. It brought Polly Howe to mind vividly. "That little Miss is gonna be a high stepper if I ever seen one," she reflected, "acts and looks jest like her Pa used to."

Edging herself up and away from the chair, Maggie weaved across the room. Pausing in front of the cloudy mirror hanging on the dingy wall over a daybed, she pushed her hair back from her face. Gazing at her reflection, she spoke aloud, "Yes, sir, I was quite a dish yet, when you was still wearing clouts, Polly. Leastways, yer Pa thought so."

Chuckling in remembrance, Maggie flung herself clumsily across the daybed and snored loudly for a few minutes.

The school bus rumbled across the road as it waddled slowly away toward the little red school that combined elementary and high school grades. Arriving there shortly later, Becky Hawk stepped down from the school bus as it stopped in front of her high school. She hurried past the group of boys that Leda Bard and Polly Howe had stopped to talk with. She flushed as the two girls glanced with amusement at her homemade skirt, which was only half as full as theirs.

"Damn 'em, they're just jealous," Becky comforted herself as she pushed open the hall door. It hadn't been easy lately to console herself when the town girls had snubbed her and the other girls from the rural and poor village where time seemed frozen in a century past. Sometimes, she hated them, hated her skimpy skirt that she had made on her mother's old treadle sewing machine, even though its blueness made her eyes look like dew-drenched wood violets and heightened the amber lights in her hair.

She remembered the first day she had worn it to school. She had sat in front of Mort Shields in English class. He had kept poking his finger in her back until she had finally turned around to ask what he wanted. "I only wanted to see your big beautiful eyes," he whispered.

"Mind your business," Becky had answered him, remembering how his father, Tom, stared holes in her every time he saw her. She remembered how Mort had waited on the school steps that same afternoon with his usual crowd and called her a pauper as she went by them. Leda and Polly had laughed along with the others as if he had made a big joke. Becky had hated them ever since.

Becky knew her folks were poor, but they weren't paupers by any standards. Her father wore out their old dirt farm along the river and managed to make a living from it. They were decent, God-fearing people, a statement Becky knew couldn't be said in all truth about some of the people around town.

"I'd like to switch places with that Leda, just once, and let her see how she'd like it in our shoes," Sarah Mann demanded with anger as she caught up with Becky at the end of the school walk right after Mort had called her a pauper.

"I wouldn't," Becky replied emphatically.

"Well, I don't like her either, but she gets everything she wants and is popular," Leda replied.

"So was her mother," Becky retorted, "especially with Mort Shields' father. I heard Ma and Pa talking 'bout them one night when they thought I was sleeping. Pa said that Mr. Bard came home one night unexpectedly and caught Leda's mother and Mort's father in bed together."

"Becky!" Sarah gasped unbelievingly.

"That's exactly how my father said it," Becky stated triumphantly. "I don't know what all happened, except Pa said Mr. Bard threatened to kill Mr. Shields. Leda's mother took on something terrible, and finally, Mr. Bard agreed to settle everything if Mr. Shields would pay him so much money. That is how the Bards got enough money to start that cattle auction market they own."

"Well, I'll be damned," Sarah had replied.

"Don't you dare tell, Sarah. I'd get in all sorts of trouble with my Pa if you do."

"Of course, I won't if you don't want me to, but that won't stop me from thinking about it every time that Leda acts so snooty."

It didn't stop Becky from thinking about it, especially this morning as she passed the snickering group in front of the school built at the turn of the century for $1,000.

It was initially a Union Free School. The school district voted to establish an academic department, and classes started soon after. To be admitted as a school under the state's Regents certification, at least five academic students were required. It was a goal that was reached quickly. Within a few years, the designation of high school came.

High school was taught upstairs, first and second grades were on the first floor in one room, and fifth and sixth grades in a nearby room. Those were all the classes that were required at the time.

Becky half-ran up the last couple of steps leading to the second-floor classrooms. Catching her toe on the last step, she stumbled, futilely attempting to hang onto her lunch pail as it flew out of her hand. She retrieved a couple of sandwiches at the feet of Prof. Ralph Tague as he posed with a stern face at the head of the stairs. Red with embarrassment, she mumbled in response to his amused, "Good morning." Half angry at him because he looked amused when she stumbled, she walked past him without looking up.

Prof. Tague turned to watch the other students as they mounted the stairs. He was a strict disciplinarian, and running up the steps was forbidden. He hadn't scolded Becky, figuring she had been embarrassed enough as it was, but he was ready to catch someone else violating the rule.

Becky's anger faded as soon as she got by the professor. She liked him mostly because he always praised her work in history class. The professor, as this teacher and others were called in those days, taught all the classes in history in the high school courses, and Becky had been in all of them. She was his best student, and he made no bones in letting the other students know about it. He always made her feel like she was important in the school. He had one child, a little girl, who was already in the first grade.

Sometimes, Becky wondered if the gossip she once heard about him was true. She couldn't simply believe that he had ever fooled around with one of his students, regardless of what high school he had been teaching in. He did have a pretty wife who was fifteen years younger than him, but that didn't make it true that he had to marry her.

The school board scarcely believed their good luck when they received his application to fill the high school's professorial vacancy six years ago. His academic achievements were above the average, and he was hired quickly. Privately, they did wonder and speculate some when they met his wife for the first time. It was very obvious that he was a great deal older than she and just as obvious a couple of months later that she was well along in pregnancy.

The professor soon proved his worth. The kids that hadn't learned or toed the mark before were doing it now to the tune of a rubber hose tap on the hands or worse, whenever the professor deemed it necessary. His type of discipline and teaching was what the school had needed for a long time. In consequence, the school board didn't give a damn if he'd had a shotgun wedding or not. The town liked and respected both him and his wife. They chose to ignore any gossip concerning his past.

Becky limped a bit as she entered the quiet study hall convened in a second-floor classroom and sat in her seat across from Sarah Mann.

"What's the matter?" Sarah whispered.

"I hurt my knee, damn it. I'll tell you about it later," Becky whispered back just as Prof. Tague entered the room. Classes were called to begin, and the students went along with their usual routine. The three hours leading to noon passed quickly. Recess came, and students made their way back to the study hall, where they ate their lunch.

"I don't see why you have to go downtown this noon, Becky," mumbled Sarah, eating her way noisily through her sandwich.

"I told you why," Becky answered impatiently. "I have to ask Doc Burton to stop by and see Ma. She's ailing again. She puked all over the kitchen when she was making coffee this morning."

"Oh, alright, come on, I'm finished," Sarah said, brushing the crumbs off her desk.

It was high noon, the sun unseasonably hot, with the sidewalk reflecting heat waves that dampened the two girls' faces as they went down the street. Dr. Thomas Burton was out when they stopped at his office, but his wife assured Becky she'd give him the message as soon as he returned. Scuffing the dust on the uneven sidewalk, the girls continued down the street.

"You know something, Becky?" Sarah asked and then didn't wait for her to answer. "You walk too damn straight with your toes pointed straight ahead like that. Don't you know you're supposed to walk with 'em slanted out a little so your fanny sways some? That's how Polly Howe walks."

Becky glanced down, then jerked her head up straight again when an amused male voice said, "No, she's walking correctly, otherwise she'd eventually get knock-kneed."

Stopped short by surprise, the girls were caught up in conversation with the stranger sitting at the wheel of his parked roadster at the curb before they realized what they were doing.

"I've been sitting here, waiting for someone to come along that I might ask directions from," the man said, smiling.

"Well, where do you want to go?" Sarah asked, losing her usual diffident manner with strangers.

"I have to get on the Gainesville-Pepacton Road," he explained. "There's supposed to be a gas shovel parked along the highway that I have to inspect."

"He must mean that piece of machinery we passed on our way to town this morning," Becky guessed, looking at Sarah for confirmation. "It's only about five or six miles from here," she added.

"In that case, as long as you know where it is, come along and show me," the man invited. "If it isn't any further than that, we wouldn't be gone longer than fifteen or twenty minutes," he added coaxingly, noting the hesitant look on their faces.

"I don't really think we should, do you, Becky?" Sarah looked at Becky dubiously.

"Oh, come on," the man wheedled. "Where's that warm hospitality you country people are supposed to show to strangers?"

Wiping the sweat from her face and imagining how cool it would feel riding in the open roadster, Becky thought, "Why not?" They'd be back in plenty of time for school. Catching sight of Mort Shields as he came out of the drug store across the street, she decided to go.

Without more ado, she climbed in beside the stranger, moving over recklessly close to make room for Sarah. Quickly moving her leg back when he shifted gears, Becky had a moment of trepidation, then forgot it as she felt the cool breeze on her face and the amazed look on Mort's as they glided smoothly down Main Street in the flashy red roadster.

"What's your names?" the stranger asked, more to make light conversation than anything else.

"I'm Becky and she is Sarah," Becky answered in a voice gone suddenly tight with the thrill and fright of what they were doing.

"You can call me 'Lucky'," their companion said, then laughed hilariously at their blank stares. Privately thinking he'd picked up a couple of lemons, he pushed the speedometer up to sixty when he couldn't stimulate the conversation beyond monosyllabic answers from the two girls.

Becky tried to protest the high speed, but the strong breeze cut off her words. The next instant, he was easing the car to a stop as he caught sight of the gas shovel parked off the shoulder of the road.

"I'll only be a few minutes," Lucky informed the girls as he got out of the car.

"Golly, I'm scared. I wished we hadn't come," Becky said as soon as he was out of earshot.

"Me, too," Sarah confided, "but we've got to ride back to school on time. Just don't let him know we're scared when he drives so fast, then maybe he'll slow down," she ended hopefully.

They watched Lucky as he inspected the machinery, making notes in a little black book as he went along. True to his word, he was finished in a few minutes and returned to the car. He slid under the wheel and let his arm fall casually around Becky's shoulders. Squirming sideways, she pushed his arm away.

"It's late and we have to go back to town," Becky said tremulously.

"It's exactly twenty minutes to one. Now that ain't late," Lucky argued.

"Well, it is for us. We have to be in school at one o'clock," Sarah replied.

"You don't expect me to believe that one, now do you? You two aren't school kids," Lucky laughed derisively.

"Maybe we're not kids, but we're still in school - high school that is," Becky said, almost panicking in fright as she kept pushing his hands away from her leg.

"Mister, we're not eighteen yet, and you sure will get yourself in a heap of trouble if you don't get us back to school right now. If we aren't there for roll call at one o'clock, Prof. Tague will notify our parents right off. The state troopers would be after you in no time flat. You wouldn't like that, now would you, mister?"

Lucky looked at Sarah sharply. She sounded either ignorant or innocent enough, he couldn't decide which, to be telling the truth.

"Well, in that case, the least I deserve is a little kiss for the ride," he said, catching Becky in a smothering embrace and kissing her brutally on the lips. White-faced, Sarah pushed down hard on the door handle and was halfway out the car when her wrist was caught in a vise-like grip.

"Get back in here, you little fool. I'll take you to town," Lucky said, pulling her back in the seat. Suddenly, he grinned at Becky. "I should have let her go, then I'd have had you all to myself. You're the one I wanted to begin with. Most of the time, I lose all conscience when I see a pretty girl with a shape like yours. I'd guess you're a virgin, too," he said, backing the car around, he headed towards town.

Becky and Sarah held hands tightly, neither breaking the silence on the ride back. Lucky pulled up to the curb and stopped the car just below the school. The two girls scrambled out of the car and dashed up the walk as if the devil was at their heels.

"Now, that is what I call gratitude," Lucky laughed as he shifted gears and wasted no time getting out of town. The last bell to assembly rang as Becky and Sarah took their seats in the study hall. The stern-eyed professor frowned at this last-minute scurrying, but for once refrained from saying anything.

Becky unobtrusively passed a note to Sarah in the next period English class. Propping it inside her notebook, Sarah read Becky's scribbled question. "What did that man mean when he called me a 'furing'? Is it good or bad?"

Sarah hastily penciled an answer on the back of the note and passed it back. "There isn't any such word, Becky," Sarah had written. "He was just making it up, thinking it would sound high-falutin' and we wouldn't know what he was talking about."

The rest of the afternoon wore on with tedious monotony as Becky tried to order her mind on her studies, but little thoughts kept slipping out, hovering around this noon time escapade. "Like barn flies around a cow turd," she restlessly thought to herself.

Glad when school was over, she hurried up the steps of the waiting bus and found a seat among the clamoring kids.

"Don't look now," Sarah said, pushing in beside her, "but the driver is watching you again."

Involuntarily, Becky glanced up and caught the bus driver's reflected face in the mirror in front of him. He smiled and gave her a big wink. She merely returned a stony look and then turned her head.

"What's the matter, Becky?" Sarah asked. "I thought you liked having him flirt with you."

"Right now, I wouldn't give a damn if I never seen another man," Becky stated flatly, "not after what happened this noon."

"It must have been awful having him kiss you like that," Sarah commiserated. "You still look pale."

"I don't want to even think about it again," Becky stated positively, "so don't talk about it, please."

Both girls seemed unusually quiet as the bus went on, stopping occasionally to let someone off. Finally, the bus lumbered to a halt at Becky's stop and with a brief "See you tomorrow" to Sarah, she left the bus and started up the farm lane.

Doc Burton was about to get in his car as Becky reached the front of the house. "Well, if it isn't Miss Becky," Doc greeted her warmly. "You're looking a little peaked today," he added, noting her pallor.

"I'm alright, Doc, except for worrying about Ma. What's ailing her?"

"Nothing that time won't cure, youngster," Doc replied. "It isn't serious," he added, seeing that Becky still looked perplexed. "In due time she'll tell you all about it. She's a mite too old-fashioned in your upbringing for me to go talking out of turn. She's going to be fine now. You just run along in and help with her chores."

Tipping his hat, he climbed into his ancient sedan and rattled down the dusty lane.

Running on in the house and not finding anyone, Becky climbed the stairs and quietly opened the door to her mother's bedroom. Mrs. Regina Hawk stood in front of the bureau mirror, gently rubbing her hand over her belly. Becky gazed at it, thinking it did look a little puffy.

"What did the doctor say is wrong with you, Ma? He wouldn't tell me a darn thing." Becky's voice startled her mother. She had yet to hear her come in. With a sort of halo look changing to a shamed flush, she self-consciously smoothed her apron down over her stomach and turned to face Becky.

"Honey, you're the most frettingest child. It ain't nothing to get stewed up about. I've got the miseries, that's all. I'll lay down a spell if you'll go out and peel some potatoes for your Pa's supper. You could put some of that salt pork on to freshen, too, while you're in the kitchen."

Feeling somewhat bewildered, Becky set about her tasks. "Maybe," she thought, "Ma has strained herself and that was what the puking was from. I'll bet that is exactly what it is. She's been working too hard again and don't want Pa and me to know it." She tripped relievedly back upstairs to her mother's room again. Sitting on the edge of the bed, she cupped her mother's toil-worn hand in hers.

"What is it, child?" her mother asked sleepily.

"Nothing much, Ma, except I want you to know that just as soon as I finish nurse's training, I'm going to make you quit working so hard. We'll get a nice apartment in the city with electricity and everything you want."

"That'll be real nice, honey, but just you pay no mind to anything until you get finished schoolin'. Then we'll talk about it. Now, run along and get supper, and I'll be real fitten by morning."

Mollified, Becky returned to the kitchen.

First the Shots, Then the Confessions

NOON BROUGHT DAILY the local news from a radio station 12 miles from Gainesville.

It wasn't much more than a ham station yet, but the valley people loved it. The announcer now interrupted his repertoire with a special news bulletin: Harold Newcomb, popularly known as "Buggie," a local resident, had shot and killed his wife in a drunken rage.

Jake Hill, owner and sole operator of his tiny restaurant, was shocked into action. Reaching for the volume control, he turned it louder. That radio had sent him into debt over $200, but it helped his business. Customers would drop in and eat a sandwich to listen to the news. Jake had hiked the prices on everything he served. His customers initially griped about it, but it was the only public place in town with a radio.

They either paid and shut up or got out. The news announcer was now recounting, in gory detail, the facts of the murder. Customers were shuffling in and out, but the restaurant filled rapidly as the announcement got around. Jake had more customers than he could handle. On his way home to lunch, he went to the door and hailed a small boy.

"Jimmy, run up to my house and tell Grace I need her to help me. Hurry now," he said, handing him a nickel.

Grace Hill opened the door in response to Jimmy's rap. Out of breath from running and excited to have a nickel, Jimmy finally managed to give her Jake's message. Thanking him, she closed the door. With a resigned expression, she stripped off her house dress and slipped her uniform off the hanger and over her head. Smoothing it down over her hips, she gazed at her reflection in the mirror. Irrelevantly, it crossed her mind that she wasn't bad-looking, not bad at all.

Her short blonde hair gave her a sophisticated look. She hadn't changed much in shape in the ten years she had been married. Reaching into the neck of her uniform, she adjusted her bra so that her well-supported breasts were held high and pointed out.

"I don't understand Jake," she mused. "There are nights when he barely bothers to look at me." She suspected he had been to Maggie's those nights, but she had never said anything about it to him. She didn't want to bring it out in the open for several reasons. He was one of the most handsome men in town, and she had loved him devotedly at one time. Now, she hated him, hated even the touch of his hand, but she kept it well hidden.

She didn't have love, but every decent, respectable woman had to have a husband, and she intended to save hers. Closing the door behind her, she walked calmly down the street. She passed the barber shop and started across the bridge when old Maggie hailed her from the open window.

"Must be yer man's real busy today, Miz Hill, you going to work and all," she cackled. "Pretty busy nights too, from all I hear."

Grace stopped involuntarily. The crazy urge to kill swept over her, transforming into a clammy, cold feeling. "How dare that filthy bitch speak to me," she silently raged, walking on.

Entering the crowded, noisy restaurant, she heard the murder news immediately. She looked at Jake behind the counter, then glanced away, afraid maybe the feeling she'd had on the bridge still showed on her face. She helped Jake for the next couple of weeks straight. The gossip about the murder died down. Buggie was being held over for the Grand Jury, and the town's morbid curiosity lessened. Jake's restaurant returned to normal patronage, and Grace stayed at home.

It was about a month later that Mr. Tomlins sold his store. Rumors pegged some foreigner had bought it and would convert it into a beer garden. If it was true, it would be the town's first and only one. There was some substance of truth in it, for a few days later, Mr. Tomlins held an auction and sold everything in the store, including a half-barrel of brine pickles, to the auctioneer. A few dried herring, plus some soda crackers, were handed out free to the crowd as an added inducement to keep them there.

By late afternoon, everything in the store had been sold to the highest bidder. With a feeling of nostalgia, Mr. Tomlins handed the building's key over to its new owner, Jhan Yevich.

The tall, dark man scrutinized the store, inside and out, mentally tabulating the renovation cost. True enough, he was a foreigner by the town's standards, but he was defiant enough right now to tell anyone that he was a United States citizen also, even if he was born of Slavic parentage. Another thing this damn town didn't know was that he had owned his own beer garden in Scranton too.

Competition had been heavy there in the red-light district, but he'd gotten enough money when he sold it to buy this place. From all he could figure out, the yokels in and around town didn't know much about anything outside this locality. They certainly didn't understand why he decided to establish a beer garden in this place or that there would be a big dam built right around here before long.

A well-known politician from New York had slipped the news to Jhan while running his joint in Scranton. The politician had been a little maudlin from too much scotch and Jhan's most attractive B-girl. Jhan initially discredited the information, but on investigating the story later, he gathered it had a grain of truth. Anyway, he sold out and bought this building.

It was a golden opportunity, and he wanted to be at the bottom. He was optimistic he'd make plenty of money when things started to boom. It might take a few months until business began to hum, but he knew the ABC law, which had nothing to do with the Alcoholic Beverage Control. It meant money collected from alcohol, bastards, and construction.

A few weeks later, Jhan opened his bar and restaurant to the public. His menu was displayed prominently in his window, embellished with the names of numerous foreign foods. The following Saturday night, he held his grand opening. He didn't expect the town's elite to patronize him, neither did he anticipate quite as many of the others that showed up. Some of the lesser notables, including old Maggie, filled the bar stools while hillbillies from all over, it seemed, ringed his tables and filled the booths.

He didn't mind the mountain boys bringing in their "gee-tars," as they called them, nor the old man who came with his fiddle. They really could make music. They played by ear, but Jhan had never heard more haunting tones. Occasionally, someone would accompany them in song. It was loud, noisy, and melodious and brought in more customers. Things went fairly smoothly, considering. He had to quiet old Maggie and a couple of her cronies a few times. Once, she had been circled by a dozen or so men watching her jig. The faster the music, the faster old Maggie danced. Egged on by the men, she whirled and pulled her skirt up to her belly button. She had never worn a pair of underwear in her life, so there was nothing unusual about it now.

Jhan didn't see anything exciting about it, but the men did. They kept singing something about "show your old muff" to the downbeat of the music as they kept time with their hands and feet. Jhan finally managed to push the men aside and make Maggie sit down.

Jhan knew he wasn't selling a helluva lot to drink; two-thirds of his crowd had tanked up on moonshine before they got there. But if his profit was small now, he knew damn well he'd make up for it later.

This was sure as hell going to be a boom town, and he'd be right in the middle of it.

Temptation Doesn't Knock—It Grabs You

"I'M GOING DOWN for the mail, Ma," Becky called from the porch.

"You just put a sweater around you, young lady," her mother called back. "It's misting out." But Becky was already off the porch, headed toward the mailbox at the end of the lane. The fine misty rain felt cool and stung her face.

"I love it," she said aloud, pausing momentarily with outstretched arms. "It makes me feel purely good." Taking a deep breath, she ran on down the lane, one with the elements.

Pulling down the flap from the mailbox, she withdrew a long official envelope. It was addressed to her in boldly typed letters. Unmindful of the rain dampening the paper, she read the letter. It was an offer of entry to the Worton School of Nursing.

Waving her arms excitedly, Becky ran pell-mell up the lane, letting the rusty screen door bang behind her as she entered the lean-to kitchen.

"I got a letter from the hospital, Ma," she shouted. "They'll accept me in training as soon as I graduate." Getting up from the table rather slowly, Mrs. Hawk set the pot of potatoes she'd just peeled in the iron sink.

"Well, now Becky, that's fine, just fine," she said. "How soon after graduation do you leave?"

"I have to be there the first of July," Becky replied.

Brushing back her damp, wispy hair, Becky's mother felt the rush of hot tears. "Damn it," she mentally cursed, "I seem to cry at the least little thing lately."

"Now Ma, don't cry. I won't go if you don't want me to."

"It's just my eyes sweating, Becky, like they always do when I sit near the heat," Mrs. Hawk assured her. She continued talking in a voice devoid of emotion.

"You know your Pa and I have waited for this day ever since you were born to us. We knew you were gonna be extra special, be a real somebody when you got grown. You just go ahead with your plans, honey. We have to find somewhere else to live anyway before too long. The damn state said they'd send us a check for this place sometime soon. We'll be all settled in a new home by the time you're done with your training, and Becky, I do want you to go. God knows you'll be better off away from here now, with all that city trash coming in here."

"I don't want to leave you, Ma," Becky said. "Not if you're still ailing. I know you're getting fatter, and I ain't seen you puking lately, but I won't go if you're not feeling well."

Turning her back on Becky, Mrs. Hawk busied herself about the kitchen, still talking. "I feel alright, Becky. You know Pa and I can take care of ourselves. You just get on to being that nurse. Heavens, child, you always were doctoring up something. Remember when you were just a youngin' and you tried to give Sarah one of them needle things with an old fountain pen? You sure would have stuck that pen point right clear in her bones if I hadn't caught you in time."

She paused a moment.

"Like you say, Becky, I am getting a mite fat, but remember when Pa killed that old sow? Well, that's what started me gaining. There ain't nothing that'll put meat on a woman's bones like a little sow belly. You just wait, honey. One of these days, your bones won't be sticking out so plain either."

With this, the conversation was dropped, and Becky started setting the table for dinner.

Gradually, June lengthened to its strawberry days, and school drew to a close. There was no time for lazy flights of fancy. Exams were upon the school, and at least for the lucky seniors, the end of high school was in sight.

For some, it was the end. They were all at the gate of higher education and possibly a more affluent way of life. Only some of the 23 prospective graduates would pass through it. They had neither the money nor the inclination to advance beyond high school.

Becky couldn't have gone on either, had the Worton Nurses Training School required an admission fee. They paid their student nurses a few dollars every month for the work they had to do, coupled with the nursing course. Becky chose it because of this reason. Her imagination ran rampant after her application had been accepted.

She pictured herself in a trim white uniform with a tiny cap perched on top of her reddish-gold curls. She'd never seen a nurse up close except two summers ago when old Doc's daughter, Molly, came home on vacation.

She was a supervising nurse in a Texas hospital and didn't get home for three or four years at a time. Doc was mighty proud of her working in that hospital. He had interned there many years before he had come to Gainesville. Becky had only seen Molly the one time when Doc took her with him on his house calls in his old rattletrap of a car.

Not even this background could detract from the dignity of Molly's stiffly starched uniform. Anyone could see Doc could hardly contain his pride in showing her off. Becky knew from that very day what she would do when she finished high school. Neither poverty nor the town's snobs would keep her from accomplishing it.

Gainesville High lost its aspect of daily routine. Students were taking their final exams and being dismissed as soon as they completed them. Becky was one of the last to finish, but she was finally done. She glanced up from her exam paper and saw there were still five students working over their papers.

She sighed wearily from tension. She was about to raise her hand to beckon Miss Mary Johnson, the room's proctor, when she saw her go up the aisle and bend over George Sutton's desk. This was the third time he had called her, apparently to clarify some question on the exam paper.

Becky suppressed a giggle as she saw the dull red mount on his face. Both the students and teachers knew he had a crush on her. He forever brought candy bars and put them on her desk in English class. She was embarrassed, but couldn't do anything to squelch him. He was only a year younger than she.

She was only twenty-two, and this had been her first year of teaching. George had never been any great shakes as a student, but then he'd had to help his father on their farm and go to school, which wasn't easy. All the teachers felt sorry for him, including Miss Johnson. They knew he'd flunk his exams this time, too, just as they knew he'd be back next year so he could see Miss Johnson. Becky finally drew her attention and handed in her exam paper. With a smile, Miss Johnson dismissed her.

At the end of the week, the school began preparing for the graduation exercises. Becky didn't get to be valedictorian or anywhere near it, but she did pass her Regents exams with credit. It was no surprise. Everyone in town knew at the beginning of the year who would be at the top of the class. A retired schoolteacher's daughter had all the requirements for salutatorian, and the son of the town's supervisor was valedictorian. She deserved the honor. Her mother had given a great deal of help, but she had studied diligently.

At the same time, the student body resented Marle, the supervisor's son, for being named valedictorian. The students all knew how he could lie and cheat as cleverly as his father, even if the faculty didn't know. There was nothing they could do about it. The teachers only had his grades, not the method he had used to obtain them.

The baccalaureate services were held in the old Methodist Church, with its spires rising staunchly above the house next door. Becky sat quietly still through the services. She had often passed by the church, but this was her first time inside.

She had never had much time for church-going. This church was patronized mainly by the more well-to-do.

Once in a while, her Ma had let her go with the Missionary Alliance people to wherever they held a meeting. They were real friendly people, poor like herself. One time, it had been real fun. One of the farmers had rigged a canopy over his truck, making it look like an authentic covered wagon from the old west. He had picked up twenty or more people who didn't have cars and taken them to a revival meeting on the other side of nearby Fishes Eddy.

They had all sat on the improvised benches in the back of the truck and sang hymns at the top of their voices. The Missionary Alliance minister was the only minister who ever came to call on the Hawks.

A high-pitched voice corralled Becky's errant attention to the choir loft. Mrs. Melissa Hopfengater, Becky knew her by sight, had condescended to sing at the exercises. She was standing beside the organ, her mouth puckered in a tiny "o," making her mustache more apparent than ever in the soft light. As the music reached a rising crescendo, all her aspirations for an operatic career were sent out in unintelligible sounds and mews. It was a small town and highly funny. Becky held her belly in tight.

"Oh, my God," she thought, "I don't dare laugh. I think I'm going to puke, just like Ma."

Catching a glimpse of Prof's face in the next pew ended her inclination to do either. After the benediction, she felt ashamed of her reaction to the singing as she marched calmly down the aisle with the rest of the class.

Two nights later, Becky proudly claimed her Regents' diploma along with the eighteen other successful graduates. Five of the seniors didn't pass their exams.

Four of them sat with woeful expressions scattered in the audience.

But not George Sutton. He looked pleased with his failure. He'd scrounged a seat in the front row directly behind Miss Johnson, rattling his program open and shut as often as he dared, trying to get her attention.

The graduates listened with polite, if little interest, to the trite speeches made by school board members who had risen magnanimously to the occasion. Having all but ignored the school's problems the year long, each member now stepped upon the podium in all his pomposity, proclaiming for all to hear his professed interest in these graduates, most of whom he wouldn't have recognized if he'd stepped on them.

The insincere thread woven in the speeches didn't perturb the audience. It merely entangled their interest with the glamor of being present at the exercises.

A week later, skillfully hiding her little silk panties in the folds of her cotton nightgown, Becky packed her cardboard suitcase. She just had to take them. They represented a smooth, silky start in a new life. She vowed silently she'd wear her cotton bloomers until she arrived at the hospital, and that would be the last time she'd wear them. She bent over and tugged up her bloomer legs as far as she could stand the elastic bottoms around her thighs.

Ma's face had turned a bright red the night Becky opened her graduation gifts, finding the silk panties.

"Burn 'em up or do something with them," Ma said. "Don't ever let me catch you wearing anything like that. They're downright shameful. Who gave 'em to you anyway?"

Becky said she'd lost the card on the box and didn't know. But she did. Miss Johnson was fond of Becky. She was pretty and young enough to know Becky would like the soft silk panties. She had also given her a tube of rose-colored lipstick. She kept it hidden in her pocketbook, but she hoped to wear some as soon as she got out of Ma's sight.

Closing the cover on her meager possessions, Becky surveyed herself again in the tiny mirror. What she could see looked nice. The white and rose-sprigged cotton dress made everything about her come alive.

A car horn tooted out in the lane. Becky grabbed her suitcase and ran down the stairs. Her excitement gave way to tears as she kissed her father and mother goodbye. She hurried out to the car parked in the lane. Doc Borton sat under the wheel, waiting to drive her to the railroad station. He looked at her and chuckled.

"Becky, you remind me of my Molly when she first went in training. She sniffled too, but in less than a week she was so happy, we couldn't have ever gotten her to give it up." He patted her arm. "You'll be the same way," he consoled. In a few minutes, Becky was asking him all sorts of questions, and Doc grinned contentedly.

Hiram and Liz stood disconsolately on the sagging stoop as they watched Doc's car send up dust swirls as it traveled down the bumpy dirt road.

"Come on, old woman. It's bad luck to watch them out of sight. Let's have a cup of tea." Laying a calloused hand on his wife's shoulder, Hiram steered her toward the kitchen door.

SOARING HIGH, PLUMMETING FASTER

POLLY HOWE OPENED her eyes, looked lazily about her room. She and kicked down the sheet that covered her, letting the early morning breeze from the open window slip over her naked body. It felt as caressing as Jim's hands, she smiled – but certainly more cooling. Remembering him there with her last night, she suddenly squeezed her thighs tightly together.

She tried to recall what it was he had called her. Finally, it came to her: "a little hot-blooded wanton," that's what it was. She admitted silently that while she didn't always understand the words Jim used, she did this time. She was a wanton alright, and right now.

Jumping quickly out of bed, she ran to the window, hoping to glimpse him by the hotel. Holding the curtain back a wee bit, she suddenly let it drop. Clamping her hand over her mouth, she made a hasty grab for the pot under the bed. She couldn't seem to bring anything up, but the retching continued for ten minutes. Wiping the cold sweat from her upper lip and forehead, she lay back on the bed.

"It's damn funny," she murmured softly. "This is three times this week I've felt sick to my stomach. I wonder if it's because Jim makes love to me too much."

Thinking of Jim, the nausea subsided, and Polly squeezed her thighs together again.

Coming out of her room an hour later, Polly found her mother downstairs making breakfast. She refused the coffee her mother poured and only nibbled on the toast on her plate. For some reason, the rich aroma of bubbling coffee made her stomach feel queasy instead of hungry.

She swallowed a bite of the toast, and without warning, nausea hit the pit of her stomach again. She couldn't make it out of the kitchen in time. Her mother supported her head while she threw up all over the floor.

"Why didn't you tell me you were sick, Polly?" her mother asked, helping her to a chair.

"Golly, Mom," Polly protested, "I don't really feel sick. I think you put too much butter on my toast. You know I don't like it," she pouted.

"Young lady," her mother commanded, "get right back to bed. I'm going to have Doc take a look at you. Come to think of it," she continued, "you have been looking a little peaked for the last couple of weeks. I can't have you coming down with something now, child. You'll be starting college in just a couple of weeks."

"I don't need a doctor simply because I've got an upset stomach," Polly answered rebelliously.

"Stop talking back to me, Polly, and do as I say."

Polly gave her mother a disgusted look and went back to her room.

Mrs. Howe cranked the wall phone a couple of turns and got Doc personally. He had just reached home from delivering a baby in Bear Hollow. It had been a complicated birth, and Doc was irate from exhaustion.

He was a little short with Mrs. Howe, to the point of being almost rude. He had tried through the years to get her to be a little calmer about Polly's simple illnesses, but hadn't succeeded.

Making another house call right now didn't appeal to him. Mrs. Howe, though, sounded so distraught, he figured he had better go. He slammed the receiver after assuring her he would be right down. He did feel rather sorry for her. She was a nervous wreck lately. She had raised Polly alone after her husband died ten years back.

He had been the valley's only veterinarian. Doc and he had been cronies of a sort. Doctor Howe had always averred there wasn't much difference between the two professions except the animals were more grateful.

Doc picked up his medical bag and went out to his car. He irritably noted that the motor hadn't had a chance to cool off yet. A few minutes later, he knocked on the Howes' door. In a distracted manner, Mrs. Howe opened the door, admitting him directly into the living room.

Patting her arm, he said, "Now you just sit down and I'll take a look at Polly. You've made her stay in bed, I suppose. You look like you have yourself all nerved up again," he observed disapprovingly.

"Yes, Polly is in bed," Mrs. Howe answered in her school-teacher manner as if her being anywhere else would be ridiculous. "After all that vomiting she's done, I don't think I'm being unduly alarmed, either."

Doc looked at her tolerantly and raised his eyebrow.

"Maybe not," he conceded, "but I'll bet it's just one of these minor summer complaints. You just sit down and I'll go take a look at her."

Reluctantly, Mrs. Howe sat down, and Doc went down the hall to Polly's room. Polly lay on her bed, a bit pale to Doc's discerning eye but looking fine. He slipped a thermometer under her tongue, grasped her wrist between his two fingers, and gave her that familiar clinical look that was part of him.

"Hmm," he mouthed unintelligibly, taking the thermometer from her mouth and reading it. "No fever, pulse normal. Just where do you hurt, Polly? Have you been eating something you shouldn't?" he questioned. Polly shook her head in mute denial.

"I don't really feel sick, Doc. My stomach has felt a little squeamish now and then this past week, but it's probably because my mother is always and forever trying to make me eat more than what I really want. This morning, she put too much butter on my toast and I puked it up."

Doc made a wry face and continued looking at her speculatively. He turned back the bed covers and gently palpated Polly's abdomen.

"When did you have your period last?" he asked bluntly. Polly looked at him blankly.

"Your sickness then," Doc explained, comprehending her blankness.

"Why didn't you say that in the first place? I don't know exactly," Polly answered. "I must have had it sometime in May, I guess."

"You guess? Don't you know?" Doc asked impatiently.

"I forgot all about it with all that I had to do at graduation time. Not having it wouldn't make me sick to my stomach, would it?" Polly questioned protestingly.

Taking in her thrusting breasts and slightly rounding belly, Doc frowned.

"Polly, in your case, I think it would. I've another examination to make first, though, before I can be certain. Now lie down flat and flex your knees. No, not like that, Polly. Like this," Doc instructed her, placing his hand under her knees, raising them up and apart.

After a swift pelvic exam, Doc raised his head and asked flatly, "Polly, who's the boy you've been messing around with? Now come on, out with it," he commanded in the face of her silence.

"You know what I'm talking about. You're going to have a baby. In about another six months, I'd say. That's why you've been having these sick spells in the mornings."

Polly's face flushed a bright pink. "Doc, it just isn't so, what you're saying. I know it isn't," she protested.

"Then it seems your knowledge is incorrect, Polly, because that, and only that, is exactly what's wrong with you," Doc stated sternly.

"I didn't mean to be bad, Doc," Polly whispered in a frightened voice, cowering as far back on the bed as she possibly could. Suddenly, she pulled the covers over her face, as if trying to blot out Doc's words.

"Polly, look at me, and listen," Doc commanded gently, pulling the covers away from her face. "You don't necessarily have to be bad, as you put it. Old Mother Nature runs her course and, given the right set of circumstances, most any girl could find herself in the same predicament that you're in. Who's the boy?" he questioned.

"I have to tell your mother, you know," he added as a stubborn expression flickered across Polly's face. "Your mother will see that he marries you, and that will be all there is to it. Now, who is the boy?"

Doc's matter-of-factness seemed to reassure Polly, and she reluctantly whispered Jim's name. Doc was sure he hadn't heard her correctly. He made her repeat it.

"Jesus to Betsy," he muttered under his breath. "Somebody ought to castrate the bastard. Did he force you or were you willing?" he asked Polly, half-angrily.

"He didn't force me," Polly said defiantly. "I thought I was in love with him."

"Love," Doc said the word disgustedly. "Lust is more like it," he thought, at least as far as Jim Hadden was concerned. He studied Polly for a few minutes.

"Jim must be at least fifteen years older than you, Polly. Are you sure you want to marry him?" he asked, churning his mind for an alternative in case she didn't.

"As far as I'm concerned, there isn't anything else to do," Polly answered tearfully. "My mother will see to that."

"I suppose so," Doc admitted. "Well, at least she won't have any difficulty in arranging it," Doc said in a tone of satisfaction. Trooper or no trooper, he could get his ass rode to hell and back for getting involved with a minor. The thought gave Doc a comforting feeling.

Commanding Polly to stay in bed for a couple of hours, Doc left her and walked purposefully down the hall to the living room and Mrs. Howe. He was prepared for a fit of hysterics and wasn't disappointed. Finally, he gave her a sedative, went back to Polly's room, and told her to call him as soon as her mother awakened.

That evening, as Jim Hadden got out of his car in the back of the hotel, he was greeted by an implacable Mrs. Howe.

Trooper Sloan, watching from his bedroom window, guessed something was up as he saw the woman's angry gestures. He sauntered out the front way and around in back barely in time to see Mrs. Howe's stiffly erect back vanish through the door on her side porch. Jim's face was red and angry, but he couldn't hide the scared look in his eyes.

Trooper Sloan glanced at him sympathetically.

"You don't have to tell me, Jim. By the actions of that old witch, I'd guess your luck has run out." Jim remained silent. "You should have known better, but then you never could pass anything up, including jail bait."

"I don't recall asking for your opinion," Jim said sullenly.

"Well, you've got it anyway," Sloan grinned. "The only advice I can give you, boy, is to make with a wedding before the Captain gets wind of this."

Jim jerked the keys out of the car switch without answering and strode angrily into the hotel.

Within a week, the town learned that Polly Howe had quietly married Jim Hadden. Some people smiled knowingly when they spoke of it, but Mrs. Howe made it very clear that she approved of the marriage, ending some of the gossip, or at least it stopped anyone from mentioning it to her.

That same week, rumors became fact when it was officially learned that both state troopers were to be stationed outside the county. Gainesville and the entire valley were to be under the control and protection of police from the Board of Water Supply.

It would be involved with the upcoming construction of the dam, never far from intruding on the lives of this little hamlet's residents.

IDEALS SINK FAST IN FOAMING BOOZE

Two men, obviously strangers in Gainesville, stood on the side-walk in front of the hotel.

The dam brought them together, not necessarily a fun trip to Gainsville.

They gazed randomly around. A few passersby looked at them curiously for the moment of passing, and that was all. Reluctantly, it seemed, the men turned, walked up the porch steps, and entered the hotel lobby. The room was sparsely furnished and, for the moment, deserted.

With a well-worn leather settee, a few hard-bottom chairs pushed hard against the walls, and set several feet back from the round center table, the room took on an air of spaciousness that belied its actual dimensions.

A desk was set behind a small counter at the back of the room. There was no denying that the huge stone fireplace, consuming over half the space of the north side, made up for the lack of decor and more luxurious furnishings. Logs sputtered and brightened as the draft caught the flames and coaxed them up the chimney. The faintly pungent odor of burning wood was not unpleasant.

Leaning on the counter, the taller of the two men reached across to the flat-top desk and flicked his finger on the tap-bell. A plump, pleasant-faced woman immediately pushed open the swing door at the back of the counter.

"Good morning, gentlemen. May I help you?" she queried.

"Yes," Mike Russo, the spokesman of the two, stated brusquely. "We'd like accommodations for the two of us here and additional quarters for six more at the beginning of next week."

With a fluttery gesture, Jennie Boyd, the hotel's proprietress, pushed the worn registry in front of them.

"Do you want singles or doubles?" She opened the book to where a pen separated the pages.

"Singles preferred," Mike requested, "but we are all men, so it won't make too much difference if you don't have them. We'll be here for some time," he added.

"We can fix you up all right," Jennie assured him cheerfully.

"Good," Mike smiled. "Now we'd like some lunch and a couple of beers. We've been on the go for hours. Can you take care of us?"

"Well, of course you can get some food here. This is a hotel. But absolutely no alcoholic beverages." Jennie straightened her spine indignantly.

"Then, just where do they serve them in this town, lady?" Mike asked with an amused grin.

With a disapproving look and a final warning that meals were served at regular hours and to be there on time if they wanted hot food, she directed them up the street to Jhan's beer garden.

"Cripes! This is going to be some helluva place to be cooped up in for God knows how long," Pete exclaimed as they headed up the street.

"You'll get used to it," Mike laughed.

Entering the beer garden, they walked directly to the bar at the end of the long room.

"Two beers," Mike ordered as the bartender paused in front of them.

"Now, this is more like it," Pete commented as he swung around on the bar stool, giving the room a cursory glance. Turning back to the bar, he watched Jhan as he deftly drew them a beer. With all the savior-faire of a keen businessman who spotted out-of-towners sharing his reasons for being the in the God-forsaken town, Jhan wiped off the bar in front of them. He set out clean ashtrays and unobtrusively squashed a cockroach climbing up the back of the bar, attesting to the the rustic environs of all kinds surrounding everyone.

"Is this the only bar in town, fella?" Mike interrogated.

Jhan nodded, drew a beer for himself, and returned to join them.

"It's the only bar," he acknowledged, "but there isn't a better one for miles around. I make it a point to serve the best in everything. Food, wine, liquor, beer. Anything you want. Name it, and you can have it. In fact, the town was dry until I opened this place a couple of months ago. Everything is done legally around here, too," he added, eyeing them warily.

"I don't remember seeing you fellows around here before. Are you local or just passing through?"

"Don't get fidgety, man," Mike laughed. "We don't give a damn if you're legal or not. When we want a beer, we want it and don't give two hoots in hell who sells it to us."

"This is the first time we've hit this town, and I, for one, hope it's the last," Pete remarked.

"Right," Mike agreed. "We're kicking the dust off this one-horse town as soon as we get this surveying job completed. There'll be plenty more, though, to take our place," he predicted.

"Is that so?" Jhan innocently asked. "Somebody find gold or something?"

"Not exactly," Mike denied, "but in a way, it's better than that. We're here to survey for the biggest dam yet to be built in the East and this town happens to be the focal point of the site."

In 1905, The City of New York, knowing more was needed for its expanding businesses and increasing population, looked to the upstate region to build an aqueduct system finished by 1924. By the early 1930s, the city won - after some contested cases - U.S. Supreme Court approval to essentially use the Delaware River to flood four rural towns and build a dam to support the structure.

Gainsville, still lost to time, knew little to nothing about these issues out of sight and out of mind.

In Gainesville, at the eastern end of the soon-to-be reservoir impounding an estimated 143,500,000,000 gallons of water to feed

New York City, construction of a dam in the $500 million project was soon to begin as the months of 1947 plodded along. New York City acquired a five-mile stretch in this valley town.

The reservoir would lie 12 miles south of the village of Delhi and would be 101 miles northwest of New York City. It would be narrow and winding, some 15 miles long and about 0.7 miles across at its widest point.

The planned 2,400-foot-long dam at Downsville would harness the largest of the city's reservoirs. Also to be known as the Gainsville Reservoir, it spread through Delaware County, New York, on the East Branch of the Delaware River in the Catskill Mountains.

Part of the New York City water supply system, it would be formed by the construction of Downsville Dam, and capture over one-quarter of the East Branch's flow.

The reservoir would be over 160 feet deep at its maximum point and would contain 430,256 acre-feet of water at full capacity. This will make it the city water system's largest reservoir by volume.

It would supply New York City with nearly 25% of its drinking water. The plan called for the water to empty into the 25.5-mile East Delaware Tunnel near the former site of one town that will be submerged, then flow through an aqueduct into the Rondout Reservoir, which empties into the 85-mile Delaware Aqueduct.

Flow will then be routed under the Hudson River into the West Branch Reservoir in Putnam County, New York, then into the Kensico Reservoir in Westchester County just north of The Bronx.

From there an aqueduct continue flow to Hillview Reservoir, from which it would be distributed by tunnel to users in the City.

Jhan knew some of these details, but he was more eager to hear what these men had to say. So he played dumb.

"You don't say," Jhan exclaimed, hoping he sounded properly surprised. "Do you mean this town is going to be wiped off the map?"

"It simply couldn't happen, man. In the first place, it isn't on the map," Mike corrected laughingly, "and secondly, our surveying is confined to upriver from here, so I presume this town will stand. Of course, there is an element of doubt until our survey is finished. When we're finished, the Board of Water Supply will have the answers to a lot of problems."

The all-powerful BWS surfacing, intruding, as so much did, in the shadow of this planned dam.

Dismissing the subject, the men ordered another beer. Jhan silently congratulated himself and magnanimously set up a free round of drinks.

The city was buying properties of the people who lived in the town, mostly underpaying these people who didn't know enough about the project to demand high prices or at least preserve a way of life families had in the hamlets for generations.

The people in town and surrounding areas became familiar with the sight of men setting up tripods, first in one district, then in another, moving from day to day to God knew where. They had heard that a dam project was to be launched, but it didn't seem imminent enough for anyone to get excited about. The people went on about their business, silent and taciturn when strangers were concerned.

There wasn't undue comment when Mrs. Boyd sold the hotel that summer.

It was generally understood she was ailing and couldn't handle the business any longer. A local businessman had offered her a tempting price, and she accepted it. In a matter of weeks, the hotel's business zoomed. Not because the quarters were made more habitable or the meals more inviting, but mainly because there was an abrupt influx of transients in town. They came and left, but the rooms were always occupied.

The surveyors terminated their work and went back to the city. On the heels of their departure came more of the Board of Water Supply personnel. Towns, farms, and all habitations within certain areas were - figuratively - wiped out of existence the day the surveyors turned in their report to the BWS.

That reality, however, would soon happen.

The upper river valley was doomed to a watery grave. State appraisers were now assessing the valley. Every inch of ground, businesses, dwellings, and everything except human life in the surveyed area, fell under the appraisers' hammer. The verdict was translated into dollars and cents to the owners. Each one who felt the board didn't offer him a fair price for his, her or their property had recourse to the courts.

A few did process their claims through this channel and discovered, "The mills of the Gods may grind slowly, but not so the courts."

Processed through legal court channels, they often found the proffered price for their possessions was lowered rather than raised. The people learned from these few examples. They couldn't fight the state, come hell or high water to the damn dam. It would be built, and it seemed nothing would stand in the way of its progress.

Actually, with the exception of the BWS, no one in the immediate vicinity knew the exact boundaries of the dam project. Some insisted it would take in Gainesville and on down the valleys as far as the Village of Centertown, with a width of three miles as the crow flies. Others had determined it would only take in the river valley above the town for about thirty miles.

Wild conjecturing and exaggerated rumors floated around town. Only gradually, as the farms and villages up the river were condemned and abandoned, did the actual site of the dam become known. Gainesville and the villages below it would remain inviolate. Some of the upper valley's hamlets would become a watery monument to the people who had lived out their lives there and to those who were living there now.

The natives who had fought the BWS for what they termed their God-given rights, now in a futile, last attempt, fought for their dead. It was with mingled horror and disbelief that they learned their cemeteries were to be emptied.

What right, they questioned, did the state have to dig up a corpse that was sleeping its last sleep?

Some were recent corpses but just as dead as those that had long ago returned to the dust as God had decreed. The old-timers vowed the state would get punished for their evil doings.

They cited a 'thing' as they called it, that had happened a few years back. As the tale went, a couple of schoolgirls and their boyfriends had taken a walk through Gainesville Cemetery just before twilight had deepened into night. It seemed one of the girls had heard there was a grave where a casket was showing through the top of the ground. It was a fresh grave, only a week old, and it was rumored that some far-off relative of the deceased had sent a floral offering, expensively unique and more beautiful than anyone had ever seen.

The girls had been curious to see it, but were afraid to go to the cemetery alone. They had coaxed the boys into going along. There had been little difficulty in finding either the grave or the floral piece.

"See! It does look like a small gate," one of the girls said excitedly. The floral arrangement, representing the gate of heaven, held the place of honor at the head of the grave. Carnations, somewhat withered and browned from the sun, entwined around its portals. The girls were utterly fascinated by its morbid beauty. The boys, callous in their youth, were disinterestedly looking about when suddenly, one pointed to the foot of the mounded grave and squealed in a high falsetto, "There's the coffin."

All eyes were pulled like magnets to where the brown earth fell away from the grave, exposing the corner of the rough box. With a sick feeling, they gazed momentarily, then as soon, turned and ran madly through the cemetery.

They only looked back once when they heard a weird hissing sound and saw a slender streak of blue flame shooting upward from the grave they had just visited. The boys corroborated the tale told by the girls. The old cemetery keeper made an investigation, but could find nothing disturbed. He covered the grave over again, though, and scolded the group for doing something unseemly, if not wicked.

The local people staunchly believed in letting the dead rest and that anyone who disturbed them would get a comeuppance. They awaited in sadness and trepidation for the ravaging of their cemeteries to begin.

The legal department of the BWS was busy for weeks with the statutes governing the removal of burial grounds. They finally cleared the way with legal papers, but the actual removal of the bodies was another story.

The head engineer phoned his New York office. "We can't hire a damn one of these yokels to help in cemetery removal. Send me a sizable crew and for cripes sake tell them what they're going to work at before you hire them. I have my regular 'skeleton crew' on the job, but not enough laborers. Hurry it along," he demanded.

The New York office hurried it along all right. They picked up a crew from the unemployed scrubs in the city, indirectly making it known that anyone reluctant to accept the job would no longer be considered eligible for welfare relief checks.

Two days following the engineer's phone call, the town's population increased by fifty or more mealy-mouthed, rough-looking characters. The cemetery evacuation began the next day.

The grave snatchers, as the local people contemptuously called them, resembled masked ghouls, wearing gowns and gloves in compliance with the sanitation code. As each tomb gave up its interred, the follow-up crew limed and filled it with dirt. Some of the graves were simply vacant holes when they were opened except for a bone here and there that crumbled to dust at the slightest disturbance and wafted gently away in the air.

When one of the novice workers drew his foreman's attention to it, the foreman smirked and asked, "Haven't you fellows ever read 'Gone With The Wind?'"

Each cemetery and every known grave in the dam's realm was finally emptied of its dead. The special enclosed vans used expressly for this purpose by the BWS carried their cadaverous burdens away to a new resting place, either to where a relative wanted it buried or to a new area the state had designated.

It was gruesome work, but it had to be done and was carried out with as much respect as time allowed.

The area of the dam was now supposedly free of dead bodies, but many of the old-timers vowed they knew plenty of graves that still clutched their dead to their bosoms. They'd never locate them for the authorities, though. New York City be damned. Let the city people drink water flavored with some of the real old pioneer stuff.

They had to admit there was nothing they could do to forestall this raping of their land, destruction of their homes, and seeing their dead desecrated, but they didn't intend to be willingly helpful. They were helpless to call a halt to the big city overpowering small hamlets where generations of families had been raised.

It was as if conquerors had arrived in some undeveloped country. That is the American way, they felt.

Run Fast Enough to Outpace the Pain

MRS. LIZ HAWK, Becky's mother, stood waiting at the end of the lane. The mail truck rumbled to a stop beside her.

"Morning, Miz Hawk. How'd you know, now, you was going to get mail this morning, and from Becky, no less?" Smiling, the mailman handed Becky's mother a postcard and a small package. "You must be right proud of your girl, Miz Hawk," he continued, "getting herself an education and all. When's she coming home?" he asked innocently, as if he hadn't read every word written on the postcard.

Mrs. Hawk turned the postcard over to read what Becky had written on the back.

"Well, she says here, it'll probably be this weekend." Hugging the package close to her breast, she started back up the lane, saying breathlessly over her shoulder, "I've a need to go, Mr. Ames. I've got bread in the oven." She thought to herself, "I'm not going to open this package and show him what's in that, too. He's always reading people's postcards and such."

The mailman drove up the road. It was true, he knew something of everybody's business. But he justified his curiosity by thinking he had to make conversation with the people on his route, and learning something of their business was a big help. He rifled through the mail on the truck seat and heard the bang of the door as Mrs. Hawk entered the house.

"She seems a little touchy this morning," he shrugged as he pondered the contents of an official-looking envelope.

Mrs. Hawk laid the package on the kitchen table and read the postcard again. "I can hardly wait till she gets here. It seems like a hundred years since I've seen her last." Opening the package carefully, she found it was from Becky. She pulled out a note tucked in the pocket of a frilly little apron.

"Ma," Becky had written, "Here's a little something for you and Pa. One of my patients made them for me. I'll tell you about it when I get home. I'll be so glad to see you both. I'm getting along fine, but I do get homesick occasionally. All my love to you and Pa." Underneath the apron was a man's white hand-stitched handkerchief with a big embroidered letter "H" in the corner.

A tear splashed down on it.

Quickly picking up the bottom of her old apron, Mrs. Hawk swiped at her eyes. The screen door banged, and Hiram walked up behind her. "Now here, what's the trouble?" he asked, taking the note from her hand and reading it. He blew his nose vigorously. "Isn't that nice of our little girl? Remembering us when she's got all that high-falutin' studying to do. You shouldn't be upsetting yourself, Liz," he said, noting her swimming eyes. "You jest lay down for a spell now," he continued.

"Remember Doc said he wanted you to take it easy. T'won't be long now before we'll be having that big boy. By the way, Liz," he added, "have you written and told Becky yet? It seems to me you oughta. Bet she'll be tickled to death, too."

Liz looked down at her husband dubiously. "Hiram, I ain't told Becky anything yet. It's sort of shameful to think about, with us being so old and all."

"Hell, woman," Hiram exploded, "the Lord seen fit to send us another little one. Now what's shameful about that? And it just ain't so, you being too old. Old women don't have babies. Let's just hope it's that boy I always wanted and stop looking askance at the Lord's ways."

"I'm sorry, Hiram," Liz said, putting her arm around him, "but these are trying days and just seem to get a body down. I'll tell Becky when she gets home this weekend. She's bound to notice something anyway. I can't pull my belly in much anymore, and wearing that old corset makes me short of breath."

Picking up the apron and handkerchief, she turned to Hiram, "Pa, I'll put your handkerchief in the top drawer of your bureau, you can never tell when you might be needing it for a funeral or something. I may as well put my apron there too. Someday when the minister comes calling again, I'll put it on."

Friday arrived at last and with the afternoon came Becky. A big car stopped in front of the Hawk's lane. Thanking the driver and simultaneously opening the car door, Becky stepped down on the rutty road. She paused momentarily as the car pulled away, enjoying the old familiar sounds and smells of the farm, then ran excitedly up the lane. Entering the house through the kitchen, she let out a whoop.

"I smell huckleberry pie, my favorite!"

Mrs. Hawk almost dropped the pie she was just lifting out of the oven. "Land of Goshen, child, you scared me out a year's growth," she exclaimed, setting the pie on the cupboard shelf.

"I'm so glad to get home, Ma," Becky said, hugging her mother. "I got so lonesome for you and Pa. Where is he?"

Hiram answered the question himself by appearing in the doorway. He lifted her clean off the floor and swooped her up in a big bear hug.

"Lands sakes, honey, but it's good to see you," he exclaimed, holding her back at arm's length. "I swear you're up and grown two inches taller and prettier than that little suckling calf Old Bell had last night."

Laughing, Becky sat down by the kitchen table. "Um," she sniffed, "everything smells so good, but Lordy, it's warm in here. Guess I plumb forgot how hot this kitchen could get when Ma goes to baking." Hiram sat down in the old wooden rocker, contentedly lighting his corncob pipe.

"Just how did you get home from the railroad station, Becky?" her mother questioned. "We didn't expect you till six o'clock tonight on that new bus."

"Well, I was standing outside the train station when a car stopped right alongside me," Becky said.

"The driver went in the station for a few minutes and when he came out he stopped and asked me if I wasn't one of the girls from Gainesville. Said I looked familiar or like that. He also told me he was a contractor here, so I decided I'd ride with him. Otherwise, I'd have had to wait over two hours for the bus."

Catching her mother's disapproving look, she added hastily, "It wasn't like he was a stranger being right from my hometown and all, besides I think he must be real rich. Said he was going to fly to California with his uncle when he finished on the dam here. His uncle owns his own airplane. Can you imagine me riding with somebody like that? Maybe he was stretching it a little, but he was real nice to talk to."

Picking up the conversation, Hiram said, "Well, guess there's no real harm to it, Becky, but it wasn't too bright of you, no matter how fast you wanted to get home. It must have been Gene Mollen you caught the ride with," he added. "His uncle is the only one that flies his own plane around here."

Reflecting a moment, he continued. "You know, that Gene Mollen's father is a senator up in Massachusetts, likewise that's what the postmaster said. Seems Gene got a letter with the senator's name and address on the back of it. Gene opened it right there in the post office and cussed a blue streak, saying right in front of the postmaster that his old man could go to hell, senator or no senator, and he'd do as he damn well pleased. Guess he's done that too, Becky, from all I hear."

"Oh, Pa, a lot of the people around here gossip just to hear themselves talk. Probably half of it isn't true," Becky commented.

"Just the same, where there's this much smoke, there has to be some fire," her father admonished her. "He's supposed to have a wife and child livin' off somewhere's too," he continued. "Some say he's divorced, but that don't make 'em rightly unwed in God's sight, Becky, and I don't want you havin' any truck with him!" he said with finality.

"I'll probably never see him again, Pa. After all, he only gave me a lift," Becky answered impatiently.

The discussion seemed to be over. The rest of the afternoon passed quickly, filled with aimless chatter. The day had been unseasonably warm but grew much cooler toward evening as the sun gradually banked its fire for the night.

"Pa," Becky coaxed after supper, "let's take a ride up around the dam works. Ma says it's changed so much up around there that I wouldn't recognize it anymore. Oh, I almost forgot," Becky exclaimed excitedly.

"I brought home a New York newspaper with me so you can read what they wrote about the dam up here. They had a big write-up about it and called it 'Doomed Valley'. I got the shivers when I read it. When I rode through town today," she continued, "it didn't seem like the same place I remembered just a few months ago. There were so many new faces on the street. If it weren't for you and Ma and this old farm, it wouldn't seem like home anymore."

"Well, it won't be much longer, Becky," Hiram answered. "The city already sent the check for this place and we put it in the bank. Come spring and we gotta vacate the farm. We're aiming to buy further up the river above the dam," he exclaimed heatedly. "If that dam ever broke, everybody down this valley for twenty miles around would drown. Go get your sweater on now, if you wanna go for that ride," he commanded, "and we'll look at that paper later."

Steering the old pick-up carefully over the bumpy auxiliary roads to the dam sector, Hiram took a deep breath and let it out slowly. "Becky," he faltered, "me and Ma have got something to tell you. I guess it's up to her to do the talking, you two being women folks and all."

Becky turned her head questioningly towards her mother. With a trapped, helpless look, Mrs. Hawk clasped her hands together nervously.

"Becky," she said, "you're a big girl now, so's I might as well put it to you straight. Remember just before you graduated when I was puking so much and old Doc wouldn't tell you what was ailing me? Well," she went on, not waiting for an answer, "I'm gonna have a little one sometime soon. Doc couldn't tell me just when 'cause I'm having the 'change' and that sorta makes him uncertain. He said it might be in January or February," she continued. "Pa and me, well Becky, we're sorta glad. With you gone we get mighty lonesome."

"Watch out girl, you'll put us over the bank!" Hiram exclaimed, as Becky hugged her mother ecstatically.

"Ma," she teased, "you didn't have to be ashamed to tell me. Besides, I already guessed it this afternoon. I didn't say anything about it because

I knew you and Pa would tell me in your own good time. I'm just about the proudest girl in the world about it."

After a few minutes of reflecting, Becky continued rather pensively. "You know Ma, when I was growing up, I got awful lonesome sometimes with you and Pa being my only kinfolks. Oh, I loved you both," she added hastily, "but sometimes I wished I had a sister or brother."

"Now Becky," Hiram interrupted, "that's the way the good Lord wanted it then and you, Ma, and me couldn't do anything about it, but seems like He's changed His mind and we're purely happy over it."

Becky reached over and held her mother's hand tightly. "Ma, it's been a long time since you had me. Are you sure everything will be alright?"

"Don't you go frettin' child. Doc said everything's fair to middlin'," her mother reproved her gently.

"There's where they're going to build a big wall for the dam, Becky," Hiram pointed out as he drove in the immediate dam vicinity. Becky's comprehension of the dam project's mechanics grew smaller and smaller as they drove on.

"It looks mighty important, Pa, but I can't even picture what it'll look like when it's finished."

"Don't feel bad, honey," her father replied. "Nobody knows what it's gonna be like 'cept maybe them that planned it. Sometimes I swear afore God Almighty Hisself, that them engineers don't know either. They're like a horde of them locusts that come over the land once in awhile," he continued vehemently, "destroying everything good and leaving nothing but bad behind 'em." With this, he turned the pick-up around and headed back home.

Saturday passed uneventfully. Becky slept until noon. After dinner, Sarah came over to see her. "Must be you kinda forgot about me, Becky," she said sulkily. "You don't write very often or are you just getting uppity with your old friends?" she asked.

"You know that isn't so, Sarah," Becky scolded. "I'm so busy I don't get much time to write."

"Just the same," Sarah thought, she is getting stuck up. Well, so was that Polly Howe, and look what happened to her. Remembering, she told

Becky about Polly running off with the trooper, growing more enthused as she gossiped on.

"Her mother keeps her mouth tight shut about the whole affair. But Polly's really showing, and everybody knows. You'd die laughing the other day, Becky," she rambled on. "Polly was home visiting and came in the A&P store for something. Old Maggie stood right next to me waiting to get checked out when Polly pushed in line ahead of her.

Old Maggie looked her right in the face and cackled, 'Well, it 'pears to me you got married just in time Polly, or have you been eatin' dried apples and drinking lots of water?' Polly's face got awful red. She didn't say a word, just checked up her groceries and walked out."

"Ma told me a long time ago that she was knocked up," Sarah rattled on, relishing the gossip she was imparting. "Now, isn't that too bad, Becky?" she gloated. "Remember how she used to snub us in school, and her no better than old Maggie all the time? Just a damn little whore."

"Golly, Sarah, you shouldn't say words like that," Becky protested. "Nobody uses that kind of language away from here. Besides, Polly's married now, and people should stop talking about her. I didn't mean to sound preachy," she hastened to say, seeing Sarah looked a little putout.

With a defiant flip of her head, Sarah got up from the rocker. "Guess I better run along, Becky. I gotta help Ma," she explained. "She is getting so uppity," she mumbled as she stalked down the lane.

"Thought Sarah was gonna sit a spell," Becky's mother sounded surprised.

"If she did intend to, Ma, she changed her mind. I think she got a little miffed at me." Becky cupped her chin in her hand and leaned her elbow on the table. "Ma," she continued, "Sarah has changed. Or is it me, or what?" She frowned questioningly at her mother.

"Maybe, Becky, but more'n likely you're the one that's changed."

Becky contemplated the idea in silence.

Busying herself around the kitchen, Mrs. Hawk took up the thread of conversation again as if they hadn't stopped talking. "Well, I'm glad you have. Pa and me can see a change in you already and we know it's all for the good. We always knew you'd be somebody someday, honey, so's you keep right on like you're doing and pay no mind to Sarah or anybody else around here. We'll miss you like all get out after you go back tomorrow, but it's all for the best, Becky."

Becky stared out the window to the fields beyond. She heard the sudden sharp blast of dynamite in the distance. Everything is changing around here, she decided.

My old school chum, the town, and even my Ma and Pa.

LOVE GOES UP IN FLAMES

HALF A MILE above the town, on both sides of the river, a new face began to etch into the terrain.

Trees that had frowned down on Gainesville's civilization for years and guarded the river road for thirty miles up the valley were pulled up by the millions. The woodchoppers from the foothills came into their glory. They were well-versed in the art of felling trees. Perhaps the city dweller considered this work unskilled and demeaning, but it was neither.

There was skill in knowing how and where to nick a tree so that it fell where a woodsman designated. If it seemed demanding to a man, it was only because he didn't hear the notes of a song in the axe ring's rhythm or see the beauty of a bird's nest woven high in a tree's branches.

The few outsiders working in the woods were a constant source of irritation to most local choppers. There was an undertone of hostility among the workers. Minor accidents occurred more and more frequently. Epithets, such as ridge runner, stump jumper and more hostile characterizations, were directed toward the woodchoppers. They, in turn, mocked and scorned their tormentors for their clumsiness in felling trees and fear of snakes in the underbrush.

The woods foreman was sure this deep-seated antagonism accounted for some of the accidents. He grew harried under the mounting tension, but finally proved to both factions that he could handle any situation in the woods. He wasn't a local man and was a novice in timberlands. Before taking this job, he had bossed in lumber camps all over Maine and Oregon.

Tall, soft-spoken, dressed in khakis, he didn't portray the typical woodsman. The play of stiff muscles beneath his soft shirt wasn't too noticeable until a particular incident. One of his crew ignored the cry of "timber." In peril of his own life, the foreman jerked him out of danger of a falling tree and then beat the hell out of him. Wiping the blood off his own battered mouth, he drew a flask of Old Grand-Dad bourbon from his hip pocket, handed it to the man on the ground, and said, "Here, have a drink." They both did, then went silently about their business.

"There's the best son of a bitch that ever walked in a pair of shoes," the crew said about their foreman later.

Hostilities were less evident after that and accidents lessened in the woods. The trees were felled, trimmed, and cut into handling lengths, then wrestled into heaps that formed rows up and down the mountain slopes. Later, they were either carted away by some of the men who could use them for fuel or they were burned on the spot. Bulldozers and diggers followed after the woodchoppers, clearing the land of stumps. The unearthed roots of the valley were loaded on stone boats - a flat sledge or drag for heaving items - to be hauled away to a dump, After, the ground was smoothed to an uninterrupted surface.

The B.W.S. relentlessly, sometimes militantly, continued construction on the dam project. Floodlights were erected in checkerboard fashion throughout the dam area, turning night into day. Work progressed on a twenty-four-hour basis. Big 'cats' whined their way up and down the runways, unloading and reloading, their cargo. Platoons of trucks were in and out of the dam sector, some carrying a warning sign "high explosives." Blasts could be heard miles around as the old was dynamited to make way for the new.

Delays that happened occasionally were tolerated with impoverished sympathy. Engineers and contractors had a goal to reach, and they would get it. Now and then, one would wire his wife in the city, "Can't make it home this weekend. Behind. Love." The wife accepted the cryptic message at face value, though she was wise enough to read between the lines. She knew that "behind" didn't always mean "behind schedule," as the message suggested, and what her husband expected her to believe.

Many behinds were attached to good-looking, amorous females following the construction jobs. Some were old pros in the business, with newer and younger ones ever swelling the ranks. They were all out for the same thing: an easy buck and a good time.

The older some of these engineers and contractors grew, the more these men hunted for whores. All a slut had to do was wiggle her behind in front of one of them, and he was after it. The older wives didn't give a damn anymore, provided their husbands continued keeping them in the style they had grown used to. The younger ones still had to learn and accept the cold, hard facts of being an engineer's or contractor's wife.

Jed Barnes, one of the head engineers, had wired his wife such a message on a Thursday morning. This time, the message was legitimate. He was working overtime on weekends and spending long hours late at night poring over a mountain of blueprints.

He was sitting at the end of the hotel's bar, guzzling beer with his assistant, Carmen Martine.

"Carmen," he said, "construction on the roads on each side of the dam area is well past the point where we've planned the core wall. I studied the blueprints, and there's one thing wrong. Granted, we could start construction of the conversion tunnel now that the roads are completed well beyond the core wall site, except for one thing. That damn tunnel has to come over another foot to the right as you're looking down at it from the North," he said.

"The depth of that rock bed we're going to drill through veers off sharply to the left, probably sixty feet. If we don't plan that tunnel another foot to the right, we'll be out of the original rock bed before we finish tunneling. I wired the B.W.S. this morning, and they've agreed to my theory. They're sending up another set of blueprints by plane in the morning. If we had gone ahead with the original blueprints, that damn tunnel would have cost N.Y.C. another million bucks. Just think of that, man! Only a misjudgment of one foot causing a million-dollar error."

Carmen grunted in admiration.

"This mistake will delay us probably a couple of days, but we should be able to start tunneling by Monday. We'll have just about enough time, at least by figures, to get the conversion tunnel completed and the river turned into it by the time winter sets in. You better get over there tomorrow, Carmen, and see that our preliminary plans are carried out."

Setting his empty glass on the bar, Carmen got up. "I'm going up to bed," he said, adding, "I know now why the men call you 'Honest Jed.' For the sake of a lousy million dollars in N.Y. City's pocket, you make me spend another weekend in this godforsaken hole."

Jed laughed.

All roads leading to the dam sector were heavily monitored the next day. Carmen directed his men with all the efficiency demanded of him. Detour signs plagued the motorists. There was too much blasting in the vicinity for the safety of anyone except the workers, and even they had to carry passes to get on their jobs.

Two days later, construction on the conversion tunnel began. The tunnel was mapped out on the east side of the core wall site, forming an arc with the terminal ends projecting from the river's bank. Just above its proposed center, a shaft forty feet in diameter plunging to a ninety-foot depth was sunk, with a huge valve filling its top terminal. Manipulating this valve would regulate the eventual water level in the dam.

A vast 'jumbo' weighing tons, resembling an octopus with its protruding drills, assembled like a scaffold on wooden tracks, drilled the numerous holes in the rock walls to dynamite the tunnel's way. As the tunnel gradually lengthened and widened, the 'jumbo' was pulled along on its tracks by an air winch, or as the workers named it, 'the tugger.'

A concreting machine constructed circular wooden forms inside the rock tunnel covered with thick concrete walls. Running just above and parallel to the tunnel, a conduit was built. It was called the control shaft. It was filled with several two-inch copper tubing that would eventually lead to a small control building and terminated in pressure gauges.

These gauges would indicate the water pressure in the conversion tunnel every twenty feet, making it possible to know and regulate the exact flow of water in and out of the dam. The state demanded that so much water flow constantly in the river. Thus, the flow would be measured.

Summer lengthened into late autumn before the conversion tunnel and its accompanying shafts were finally completed. The day was nearing for the "turning of the river." The valley residents were still speculating as to how a river that had run its natural course for hundreds, perhaps thousands of years, could be forced by a man's hand to flow in another direction. Feats they had termed impossible had been accomplished daily in front of their eyes, and most of them were employed on the project. Still, they couldn't believe the river could be turned by many tunnels and gadgets. It was too technical for any layman to comprehend fully.

The day did arrive, however, when the engineers were ready to divert the river's course through the conversion tunnel, bypassing the core wall site and veering its way back to its original channel below. They had grown so used to hearing the process spoken of as "turning the river" that they spoke of the crucial time as "T-Day."

"T-Day" dawned cloudy and depressing, but that didn't deter the curious onlookers from all over the valley, who crowded at every vantage point.

A flare went off, signaling the watchman at the control shaft to activate the mechanism that pulled out the shaft's plug.

The crowd waited in hushed expectancy for some disaster. There was none. Slowly, smoothly, the big Delaware River, like a fickle lover deserting his - or her - love, veered its course to the right, down through the conversion tunnel and back into its original course below the core wall site, leaving two hundred feet of mud and debris in its former bed to the left.

Jed looked exultantly at Carmen as they stood alongside the conversion tunnel.

"We made it, man!" he shouted. "Ahead of schedule, too."

"Just in the nick of time, by the looks of the sky," Carmen retorted. "In fact, it's starting to spit a little snow right now. Looks as if we're caught up here for the winter." He simply couldn't keep the elation out of his voice. Jed glanced at him a little humorously. "You know, Carmen," he said, "you can go on back to the city this weekend if you choose to, but me, no. I must wire my wife in the morning. I can't get away for another couple of weeks."

"You better be careful, you old whore-master," Carmen cautioned him affectionately. "Between the booze and that bottle-assed redhead, you won't be able to get back at all. You ought to know by now that you can't race an old motor."

"Now let me tell you something, fella," Jed retorted. "It's been said that a change of pasture fattens the calf, and I'm about to find out if it's true."

Laughing, they left the dam site together.

A Historical Remembrance - Construction of the Actual Pepacton Reservoir and Downsville Dam

1947-1954

CITY OF NEW YORK
BOARD OF WATER SUPPLY
PERTINENT DATA
PEPACTON RESERVOIR
AND
DOWNSVILLE DAM

BOARD OF WATER SUPPLY
CITY OF NEW YORK
PERTINENT DATA
Length of Dam at Elevation   2,450 feet
Max. Height of Dam Above River Bed 204 feet
Storage Capacity (Billion Gallons) 147
Watershed Area (Sqa. Mi) 372
Lent of Reservoir (Miles) 18.5
Villages Submerged 4
Cemeteries Removed 10
Permanent Population Displaced 943

Groundbreaking June 20, 1907 for New York Aqueduct and Reservoir System (NYC Water via Flickr)

1947 Pepacton Reservoir Carpenter Crew (Colchester Historical Society)

Construction began on the dam in 1947.
(Colchester Historical Society)

Building the dam required detailed and hard-labor work. (Colchester Historical Society)

Downsville Dam diversion tunnel looking east in December, 1948, as blasting through rock was occurring. (NYC Water via Flickr)

March 6, 1957, photo of waste channel with Pepacton River Reservoir in the background. (NYC Water via Flickr)

RIVERS TWIST, PEOPLE DISAPPEAR

"**H**IRAM, I'VE BEEN getting awfully fidgety these past few days," Liz Hawk said.

"I just can't seem to sleep at night lately. Don't know if it's because I'm missing Becky or what. Let's go for a ride up where they turned the river," she added. Laying her hand on his shoulder, Liz looked at her husband imploringly.

"Well now, go take off your apron, Liz, and we'll do just that. You sure you're up to riding over that bumpy road, though?" he asked worriedly.

"Sure and certain," she reassured him.

"How much longer do we have to wait for that boy, Liz? Didn't Doc say yet?" Hiram watched as her belly quivered beneath her apron.

"Could be a month, give or take a few days," Liz replied. "Come on," she urged, slipping on her jacket. "Maybe a few bumps will hurry it along. Besides, I feel like getting out of this house for a spell."

Backing his old pickup out of the barn, Hiram headed it up the old river road.

"We should have brought our fishing poles," Liz remarked after they had gone a couple of miles. "See that groundwater up ahead? That's a good spot for bullheads, and I know it. It's so close to the road we could have fished right alongside the truck."

Almost opposite the groundwater, she continued, "Now wouldn't you think the B.W.S. would put a fence along here? It's downright dangerous."

"Liz, that groundwater is just a side flow from the river underground. It ain't more than five feet deep with a lot of mud on the bottom. Why, even a tadpole would be ashamed to be caught in it."

"Well, it ain't safe to drive along it, the way I see it," Liz answered.

Five or six miles up the road, Hiram stopped the truck and pointed his finger out the window. "Right over there, Liz, where you see that heap of dirt is where they started dynamiting to turn the river. Just this side is two or three hundred feet of the old riverbed. You can't see too much of it now. It's getting too dusky out," Hiram explained.

"Glory be, Hirmy," Liz said, using a pet name for him she hadn't used for years, "do you ever stop to think how mortal man has changed the Lord's handiwork in these parts? Even the people have changed," she continued without waiting for an answer.

"Such goings-on I've never seen before. Seems like a lot of the womenfolk are taking up with these dam workers. Two or three have run off with them too. Why, Hiram, the other day Mandy Comfort was telling me that one of those men working on the dam, he's from Alabama," she elaborated.

"He up and took off with Mat Stillwell's young girl. Took her clear to Pennsylvania somewhere, and she's only fourteen years old to boot. Guess he's got himself in a peck of trouble, her being underage and all. State troopers have been looking for them, but guess they haven't caught up with them yet. You know, Hiram, I miss Becky something awful, but in a way, it's best she ain't around here. There's no telling sometimes how those outsiders can work on a young girl."

"Liz, honey," Hiram laughed, "you're just bursting with talk and gumption. Guess I better get you home. Bet that boy of ours will come knocking tonight."

"This here ride just plumb did me good, Hiram. But take those chuckholes easy," Liz answered, squirming a little.

"O.K. but you close that window," cautioned Hiram. "You'll catch your death of damnation sitting there in that draft."

"Just listen to those peep toads hollering, 'tis a sure sign winter ain't far off. Those peepers can sure make a body feel lonesome, can't they, Hiram?" Liz paused a minute to listen as she rolled up the window.

"Well, yes, Liz. I suppose so," Hiram admitted after a moment's reflection. "Then again," he continued, "they can make a man feel purely content, like I do."

"Hiram, watch it!" screamed Liz as a big 1942 Chrysler Town & Country station wagon came careening up the road. "He ain't gonna give us room to pass, he's driving drunk for sure."

Hiram jerked the wheel of his truck to the right, missing the oncoming car by inches. The pickup hit the loose gravel on the road's shoulder and went into a skid. "My God, Hiram, the groundwater," but Liz's words were muffled as she was hurled against him when the truck rolled over with its top resting on the groundwater bottom, the muddy water swirling around and partly covering it.

An hour later, the B.W.S. patrol car, on its routine patrol of the area, spotted the partly submerged pickup.

"Cripes," the driver exploded, "looks like some fool has turned his car upside in that hole."

Getting out of the patrol car to investigate, John, the driver, cursed under his breath. "Frank," he said to the other patrolman, "they sure hit that water hard. Look at these skid marks."

"Looks that way," Frank confirmed. "Let's take a look in the water. It's not too deep to wade along here."

"It might not be deep, but it's sure cold as hell," John shiveringly replied, stepping tentatively into the groundwater. Holding onto one of the truck's wheels for support, he probed under the water for the door handle. "Yike," he yelled, bringing his bleeding hand up quickly.

"That glass is broken in the door, and the door's jammed. I can't open it. Cut my hand," he explained laconically to Frank. "You set up a couple of flares and stay here. I'm going to town for help and get my hand attended to. One thing's for sure," he added, "there's someone in that truck alright. I had a hold of a person's hair, but whoever it is, isn't alive by now."

In less than an hour, the two bodies were extricated from the truck's cabin. Old Doc stood by just in case, by some miracle, there might be some sign of life left. He pulled his stethoscope from his ears, leaving it to swing like a pendulum from his neck. Straightening up from examining the two bodies, he said to no one in particular rather wearily, sadly, "They're gone, the three of them."

"Three, Doc?" John puzzled, supporting his bandaged hand as he bent down to look at the bodies.

"Yep, that's right," Doc reaffirmed, picking up his bag. "Liz Hawk was expecting most any day now. Better let me notify the next of kin," he added as an afterthought. "I'll take care of it as soon as I get back to the office."

ASHES IN THE WIND, HOPE ON THE RUN

BECKY SAT ON the edge of her cot and slipped off her shoes. "Damn," she groaned softly as she pulled her feet up and started rubbing them. Hearing a faint squeak, she glanced up to see her door opening slowly. "More tricks," she thought exasperatedly, "and me dead on my feet." Suddenly, the door was flung open. Three of her classmates burst, giggling and tumbling recklessly onto her bed.

"Room gal, give us some room," one of them giggled as they pushed Becky over.

"Hey, take it easy," Becky protested as she straightened up.

"Golly Hawk, what gives?" Aldeen questioned. "You look like you got the doldrums, or should I say 'the miseries' as you so aptly put it?"

Becky looked at her speculatively. "She's the cutest of the whole class," she thought irrelevantly, then answered her question. "Nothing is the matter except this being on my feet for twelve hours today makes them feel like clementines."

"Well, let's scatter the patter, chums, and make her feel better," Aldeen suggested. Interrupting each other, tripping over words in their haste to enlighten Becky, the girls finally told her the news. Becky eyed them suspiciously.

"What, a repeat?" questioned Aldeen dramatically. Jumping up on a chair and assuming the demeanor of a town crier, Aldeen enunciated vibrantly. "Hark ye! Hark ye! Our little ole class has come through the first months of grueling days and sweating palms called probation. Monday, we get those little coveted white caps pinned on our hair and become the cutest third-rate humans again."

Stepping down dexterously from the chair, she continued talking. "It ain't fittin', as Hawk used to say, to tell the bad with the good, but good or bad, here goes. Neither Hallock nor Jones made the grade. Not enough gray matter, I guess. It's too bad," she commiserated without sympathizing with the statement.

"How do you know all this, Aldeen?" Becky asked dubiously. "It hasn't been announced officially that I know of."

"Oh, I've a cousin who's a friend of the super," Aldeen bragged a trifle smugly. "It's supposed to be top secret yet, so don't go squelching," she cautioned. "Leave it 'status quo' between us here."

"Well, I was certainly expecting to make it," Becky stated flatly, "but then," she added, "it's real, real nice to know that I did and that the rest of you did too. Now, get the heck out of here and let me get some rest. After that trick of short-sheeting my bed last night, you girls ought to rock me to sleep. I never," she broke off laughingly, then continued, "I promise I'll go in a sweat with all of you tomorrow."

"Not you all, Hawk," Aldeen corrected, "all of you. I swear you could still brush hayseed out of your corn-silk hair."

"That's for sure," teased one of the other girls. "Remember when old grim-face Allen was teaching us to take temperatures, Hawk?" she needled, opening the door. Becky's face flushed crimson as they went out, not waiting for her to reply.

"Remember," she muttered, "how could I forget?" Embarrassment washed over her again as she recalled that particular day. When it had been her turn to insert the rectal thermometer, she had asked Instructor Allen, "What do I do, just poke it in?" The class had been reprimanded severely by Miss Allen for laughing at Becky, but there had been a twinkle in her own eyes as she patiently explained it to her.

"Miss Hawk," she had said primly, "perhaps your quaint expression means the same, but in medical terminology, the word is insert, not poke."

Her expressions were not only quaint, Becky discovered, but strictly native to her home locale. After arriving in the city, she recollected the first time she and Aldeen had gone shopping downtown. Becky had made a few small purchases in one of the department stores and stopped at the checkout counter to pay for them.

The cashier pushed them across the counter individually toward Becky as she tallied the cost. Becky paid her and asked her to put the packages in a sack. The cashier looked completely bewildered until Aldeen interrupted that Becky wanted them put in a paper bag so she could carry them.

"Either I'm dumb, or she is," Becky remarked to Aldeen on their way out of the store.

"You're not dumb, Hawk, neither is she," Aldeen comforted her. "But you are a typical little hillbilly," she laughed. "I guess you'll learn though, kid," she added, not unkindly. And she had.

Stifling a yawn, Becky went over to her desk, smiling at her remembered embarrassment. She gazed down at her class notebook, opened it, and flipped it shut again. "I'm too weary to study," she thought. "Besides, I wouldn't know an ass from an elbow tonight." Unbuttoning the stiff white collar from her probie's uniform, Becky laid it on the dresser, then impulsively picked it up and held it banded on top of her head. Preening this way and that to get the full effect of the improvised cap, she exclaimed softly, "Just wait until Ma and Pa see me in the real McCoy."

An authoritative rap on her door disrupted her thoughts, pulling her away from the mirror. Throwing the collar back on the dresser, she hurried to answer it. Mrs. Louden, the house mother, stood there.

"Miss Hawk, you're wanted over in Dr. Bentley's office immediately. No, I don't know what he wants," she replied to Becky's inquiry. "But hurry, dear," she admonished. "He sounded imperative, so it's probably important."

"Thank you," Becky replied, "I'll go right over."

"Why would Dr. Bentley want to see me after I'm off duty," she puzzled on her way to his office. Then she recalled seeing his name on the bulletin board under "officer of the day." "Probably, he wants to chew me out over something I did or didn't do," she conjectured, reminding herself what a stickler he was for rules.

If somebody fractured one, he didn't seem to mind what time of day or night he called them on the carpet. Every student in the present class had, at one time or another, incurred his displeasure and subsequent reprimanding. She shivered.

Dr. Bentley opened the door himself at her hesitant rap. He motioned her to a chair but remained standing himself.

"Miss Hawk," he said directly, "I understand you're quite alone in the world except for your parents. Is that right?"

"Yes, sir," Becky replied meekly. "I do have a cousin of my mother's in Buffalo but I don't remember her at all," she added.

"No special friends?" he inquired.

"Just the neighbors at home, Dr. Bentley, but no one very special. Why?" Becky asked bluntly. "Have I done something dreadful or what's wrong, Dr.?" she demanded, half rising from her chair.

"I've probably gone at this all wrong, Miss Hawk. Please forgive me. I was trying to find out if there were someone close to you to help ease the shock of my news. There's no easy way to tell you, my dear, or I would seek it out. Your parents were killed in an accident a short time ago. Dr. Borton from Gainesville just phoned me. They were on –."

The rest of his words faded out when, for the first time in her young life, Becky fainted.

A short time later, Becky regained consciousness and looked dazedly around. Mrs. Louden was hovering anxiously over her. Dr. Bentley emerged from the doorway and handed her a glass of pink liquid.

"Drink this," he commanded in a gruff voice. "I'll drive you and Mrs. Louden back to your room and you lie down for a couple of hours," he continued. "By then, Dr. Borton will be here. He's going to take you home. He said you were to stay with him and for you not to worry. He'll give you all the details when he arrives.

"Also," he added, "I've taken care of your leave of absence from the training school. Just notify us when you're ready to return."

"My dear," he continued softer, patting her hand, "I will admit this is a terrifying ordeal for you, but try to remember this. As a nurse, you will cope with untold suffering and pain. God's ways are inexplicable. Perhaps this is His way of making you a very special emissary of your profession. Your words of comfort and consolation to others will not be empty and meaningless. They will stem from personal suffering and eventually hold the antidote for your own grief."

Becky's eyes dilated with shock and the effects of the sedative the Doctor had given her. Her brain was recording the words Dr. Bentley was saying somewhere, but she couldn't seem to make sense of them. There was a dull throb in the back of her head. It wasn't until hours later, on her way home with Doc, that she began to feel the full impact of tearing, wrenching grief.

Huddled in the corner of the seat beside Doc, she whimpered like a hurt animal. Doc's eyes wavered between Becky and the road. He drove the car at a steady, moderate speed. He was worried. "I've got to make her cry," he thought. "Really cry and wash away some of that pain and shock."

With pity in his heart, he asked deliberately, "Did you know your Ma and Pa had intended to name that new baby after me, Becky? That is," he chuckled, "if it was a boy. It made that baby kind of special to me. It makes you special with me, too, Becky, being your part and parcel of the whole lot." Doc glanced sideways momentarily to see the effects of his words, then continued.

"Your Ma made mention just the other day in my office, Becky, of how well you were getting on in training. I've never seen two people more rightly proud of their daughter than your Ma and Pa were."

"Doc," Becky cried out, "they'll never see me in my new cap or a real nurse's uniform now. They'll never..." Breaking off in mid-sentence, she sobbed uncontrollably.

As he continued driving, a mingled expression of pity and satisfaction crossed his face.

When Doc arrived home, his wife put Becky to bed. A few minutes later, he returned to the room and handed Becky a small yellow capsule with a glass of water.

"Swallow this dear," he instructed. "It'll help you sleep. We've a lot of things to attend to tomorrow."

Almost immediately, Becky drifted off into a deep, dreamless slumber.

Looking pale and listless the next morning, Becky listened as Doc explained that he had been officially appointed administrator of her affairs until she was twenty-one.

"I've checked your parents' financial affairs and found they deposited a check for $3,750 in the bank last October. It was a check from the B.W.S. in full payment of their farm. It is all they had of any material worth, Becky, and of course it's yours now, after everything is settled."

"Of course, you know the cemetery was condemned here in Gainesville. The nearest one now is at Ralton. What do you propose to do about the burial?"

"Doc, I've been thinking it over since early this morning. This may sound awful to you, I know it will to the town, but I want my parents cremated."

"Are you sure you've thought this over well?" asked Doc, giving her a startled look.

"I'm sure," Becky replied, and she continued. "Please don't make me go and see them now. I want to remember them as they were when I left them the last time." Her voice grew soft and husky as she continued.

"They were standing at the end of the lane after kissing me goodbye. Pa had his arm around Ma's shoulders, sort of like he was loving and protecting her at the same time. Ma's eyes were full of tears, but she smiled at me all the same. I want this to be my last memory of them."

"Becky, child, tell me," Doc demanded, "how did you arrive at this decision? There's so little of this type of burial in these parts. None, in fact," he added, "that I've heard of in a radius of thirty-forty miles. It does seem strange," he offered, looking at Becky closely.

"All I know about it, Doc, is from reading an article on it in a magazine," Becky stated matter-of-factly. "It was all about the overcrowded cemeteries in New York. It stated there would come a day when people would, by way of necessity, have to cremate their dead. It sounded simple and right."

"Don't you understand, Doc?" she pleaded. "I can't bury them in a strange cemetery miles away from here. Here is where they've always lived. They were born here. They'd turn over in their graves if I took them away from here now. Why, with the city taking their farm, it took the heart out of them. Just thinking about having to move. I could tell. Now, it's finally taken their lives. Yes," she explained passionately, "indirectly, that damn city claimed their lives."

"Now take it easy, honey," Doc said quietly. "We'll do whatever you want, of course. It won't cost any more or take any more time or effort." Rising slowly from his chair, Doc patted her on the head. "I've a few sick calls to make this morning, Becky, and I'm a little late, so I've got to get on. The minister from the Missionary Alliance Church is coming over this morning. Said he was your folks' minister, that right?" he questioned. Becky nodded assent. "At least," she modified, "he was the only minister that ever came to see us."

"It must be him now," Doc said as a car stopped in the driveway. "You tell him what you want to do, Becky, and between us, we'll take care of it."

With this, he picked up his bag, stopped to chat a minute with the minister outside, and left to make his morning rounds.

A week later, Becky was on her way back to the hospital. She was pale but composed. She carried the memory of Dr. Borton's kindness and generosity, as well as the comfort and tranquility of the minister's prayers.

But what sustained her, Becky reflected, no one knew except herself and Gene Mollen. No one knew how she had scoured the town for Gene two nights ago, finally finding him staring down into a glass of liquor as if seeing things in its golden amber depth. He had no difficulty in recognizing her.

"You're the young lady I gave a lift to from East Branch some time ago," he stated rather than asked. "What's on your mind, honey?" he questioned. "You don't look like one of these bar-hopping flies. Sit down," he invited.

"Now that I've found him, I'm scared to death," Becky thought, trembling at her audacity. "I'm scared of him and scared to tell him what I want." Still standing, she asked tremulously, "Mr. Mollen, can we go somewhere to talk? Not in here," she shook her head negatively as he started to pull out a chair. "I want to talk to you alone."

"Sure, doll," Gene said, getting up from the table. "Come on over to my trailer," he added, eyeing her appreciatively. Taking mental note of his somewhat unsteady gait, Becky desperately followed him out. "You're not drunk, are you, Mr. Mollen?" she asked directly once they got outside. "Because this is business I want to talk to you about, strictly business," she continued, "and another thing, before I go in that trailer, I want you to know you are right about one thing. I'm not like one of those barflies as you called those girls in Jhan's. This is business," she reiterated.

"Now honey, you get this straight, too," Gene replied roughly, "you said you wanted to see me. Well, I'm for the seeing, and as for going in that trailer, I suggested it only because you were so concerned about us being alone. And here's one for the book, yours or anyone else's," he continued with a belligerent tone.

"I'm not drunk and I don't mess around with jailbait." With this, he opened the trailer door and mockingly bowed her in.

Seated across the small room from Gene, Becky felt somewhat abashed and found it hard to begin. Finally, hesitatingly, she said, "Mr. Mollen, you told me that day I rode home with you that your uncle owned an airplane."

"Must be I did," Gene acknowledged, "because he does."

"Is he around here?" Becky questioned. Gene looked at her skeptically before replying negatively.

"What do you want of him anyway, girl?" he said after a moment. "Quit stalling and out with it."

"Mr. Mollen, please don't be angry with me," Becky pleaded. "It's just that I don't know anyone else who has a plane, and I have to hire one for just a little while."

"Do you have to go somewhere fast, Miss Hawk? It is Miss Hawk, isn't it?" Gene asked. Interrupting her as she started to speak. "Now, I remember where I heard that name just recently. They were your parents that were killed in that accident a few days ago, right?"

Nodding affirmatively, Becky said, "That's right, Mr. Mollen. Their death left me an orphan," she continued. "I have no near kin and I need your help. I do have some money, though, left from what the B.W.S.

paid my parents for their farm. It's not too much," she added, "but I think it's enough to pay for what I want done."

Leaning forward slightly in her chair, Becky continued when Gene failed to comment. "I don't know if you'll be shocked at what I've done or not, but it was the only thing to do," she added defensively. "Yes," Gene encouraged her, "go on."

"I had my parents' bodies cremated," she stated in subdued tones, then waited for some sign of disapproval from Gene. There was none except a matter-of-fact, "Oh?"

"I couldn't have them buried in a strange cemetery, miles from here," she explained, her voice edged with tears. Controlling herself with effort, she withdrew an urn from her handbag. "I want to scatter their ashes over the farm they loved. That's why I want to hire a plane," she explained, bursting into tears.

Gently, Gene extricated the urn from her trembling hands and gazed at it thoughtfully. Placing it on a small table, he turned back to her.

Completely sober, he said gently, "Honey, I don't know. I just don't know. Maybe we'd be breaking some kind of sanitation law or something. I've done just about everything in my life, but nothing like this."

"As for my uncle, now that I know what you want with him, I'll tell you about him."

"He'll be here tomorrow afternoon. As for hiring him to do something like this, he wouldn't even consider it. In the first place, he's got plenty of money and in the second, he's sort of a stuffed shirt for all his helling around," he explained.

"Granted, I'm his favorite nephew, but not even for me would he chance sullying the Mollen name. He's still my father's brother and my father is a U.S. Senator," he added.

Gene then grinned devilishly.

"You'd never guess I come from a fine old family, would you?" he asked. "And I'm the current black sheep. Also," he said, wagging his finger at her, "if you think things around this part of the country smell, you should whiff the brew from the political pot my family stews in."

"I'm sorry, Mr. Mollen," Becky said by way of an answer. "I thought you could help me, but I guess you can't."

Shedding his jocular manner, Gene turned thoughtful for a moment.

"Honey, maybe I can at that," he finally admitted. "It's true my uncle wouldn't hear of it, but that's not saying I won't help a fair damsel in distress. I've flunked out of a lot of things in my life, but my pilot's test wasn't one of them. In fact, I did four years in the U.S. Air Force. I flew those big babies to hell and Harlem and back again," he bragged.

"Uncle Jim lets me have the feel of the joystick every time he comes here. Just says he doesn't want me to get rusty, but what he really wants is to get me interested in an airfield he's promoting. Guess this business I'm in just doesn't have enough shine and polish to suit the senator's taste, so my ever-loving uncle is trying to ameliorate things," he acknowledged with some bitterness.

He poured himself a straight whiskey. "I'd offer you one, Miss Hawk, but I must keep it within the law. You know, minors and all that stuff, but here's to you anyway," he said, waving his glass as he downed it in one gulp.

"Well, for your information, Mr. Mollen, I'm past eighteen, but I still don't drink," she said flatly as he made a motion to pour her one.

"So be it," Gene laughed.

Becky got up and put the urn in her bag. Gene made a protesting gesture. "Just a minute, honey, let's get down to business - your business," he emphasized. "Now, you meet me at the end of Main Street tomorrow night at seven o'clock. I'll pick you up in my car, and we'll go down to Hennsey's flat from there. That's where Uncle Jim keeps his plane. From there, we'll fly wherever you want to."

"One more thing," he added, halting her as she started to leave.

"Now I don't know just how legal or illegal it may be," he said, "sprinkling dead people's ashes over the land, whether it belongs to them or the B.W.S. Still, if you tell anyone about this, you just might get your pretty self in a heap of trouble, as well as me."

Crossing her heart like a little girl, Becky reassured him. "Mr. Mollen, I promise I'll never tell anyone, no matter what," she said earnestly.

"Okay, kid, get going," Gene commanded, holding the door open. Raising herself slightly on tiptoe, she kissed him softly on the cheek and then ran down the steps.

Gene stood momentarily in the doorway, watching as she fled across the trailer lot.

"Gad!" he exclaimed, rubbing his hand carefully over his cheek. "Doesn't she know what a chance she took coming here like that? Somebody ought to tell her that nature didn't intend for man to let his seed go to waste," he muttered.

He felt the cool air ruffle his hair. "That's it," he exclaimed, "she's like a breath of fresh mountain air. Air like this little town used to breathe before it was polluted by this confounded dam project."

"Man!" he protested as he peeled off his clothes and got into bed. "Virgin territory," he kept mumbling in his restless sleep.

The next morning, as he got out of bed, he gazed down at a yellowish stain on the bed sheet. "Cripes," he cursed softly, "I did it again."

The town had grown accustomed to the sounds of the dam machinery and the accompanying blasts of high explosives. They took it in their stride, but the drone of an airplane, always to man, woman, or child, pulled their gaze skyward. True, more planes were flying over the valley now than ever before. Still, they never seemed to become common with the inhabitants.

Twilight approached with darkness close behind. Pedestrians paused on the streets of Gainesville while others stood on their porches or any vantage point they might have to watch the plane now circling low and wide between the town and the nearby hills. It wasn't far off, at least by air miles. It was like a giant bird as it swooped and tilted.

In that plane, Becky sat in the cockpit beside Gene. Neither thrilled nor frightened. It was her first time in the air, but it was far from her mind.

"Do it, now, Miss Hawk," Gene yelled above the roar of the plane's motor as he made a swoop over Becky's old home. Bringing the plane up and leveling off in a graceful maneuver, he looked at Becky's wind-swept hair and pale face, then down at her hands.

"Mission accomplished?" he asked, then let out an explosive breath. "Where's the urn?" he asked, knowing the answer. "I dropped it too, Mr. Mollen. I didn't mean to, but the wind forced it out of my hand," Becky quavered.

"Dear God and all the saints!" he exclaimed. "Baby, all we needed to do was drop that thing on somebody's head, and we'll lose our own." Cursing softly, he circled the plane low again. "Well, as far as I can see, there doesn't seem to be anyone around down there. It looks pretty dead, so I guess there's no harm done. It's sure smashed to smithereens by now."

"I'm sorry, Mr. Mollen," she apologized again. A low rumble started in the east. "Say, that sounds like thunder," Gene said. "You don't get rain here at this time of year, do you?" he asked.

"Sometimes," Becky replied. "It's never much, just a warning that real cold weather is about due."

"At any rate, we better get this crate back on land before Uncle Jim comes looking for me," Gene said jokingly.

Minutes later, he lifted Becky from the plane at their take-off point. They made a quick dash for the car as the heavens opened wide, sending down a torrent of rain.

"Thought you said it wouldn't be much," Gene laughed, wiping his face dry.

"It usually isn't, Mr. Mollen. It's a good omen," Becky murmured.

"You remind me of a soft spring morning, Rebecca," Gene said impulsively, using her given name for the first time as he started the car. Becky remained silent and reflective as they rode back to town.

"You didn't tell me how much I'm supposed to pay you for this, Mr. Mollen," Becky stated as he stopped on Main Street to let her out.

"Honey," he said, "if I've helped save your dream or build a new one, that's all the pay I want. Maybe someday we'll meet again. If we do, I hope you're still holding onto a dream. No matter how old you are, remember that dreams and hopes are ever the revitalizing factor of a happy life," he said.

There was a pause before he added, "I haven't any," in a reply to her questioning look. With a mock salute, he drove off.

She now had another mission to accomplish. Back to nurses' training.

The screech of the train's brakes brought Becky out of her reverie. Lifting her bag down from the rack above her, she made her way out and off the train now far away from Gainsville.

She hailed a cab. "Worton Hospital," she announced cryptically to the driver as she settled herself in the seat.

A NEW TOWN, A NEW VICE, A NEW MISTAKE

THE PEAK OF a boom was casting its shadow upon the town.

Slowly and inexorably, Gainesville was forced to accept its destiny as another boom town. It was definitely on the map, with its importance related to that of the dam. These days, people didn't hail each other on the streets in camaraderie. Two-thirds of the pedestrians and motorists were strangers the locals didn't know. The town was bursting at its seams with them, and everywhere one went, it was crowded.

Jake Hill didn't have to turn on his radio now to lure in customers. His restaurant was filled to capacity most of the time. Business was so heavy that he hired a counterman and eventually demanded his wife work steadily too. He had to admit that right from the start, she had been a damn good drawing card. He even took to wondering sometimes if he could be getting just a wee bit jealous of her.

He hadn't particularly noticed her shape these past few years, but looking at it now through some of his customers' eyes, it didn't look bad, not bad at all. He watched her swish up and down the counter and among the tables in her new fitted uniform. The curve of her hip undulated sensuously—just enough, Jake thought, to give any red-blooded man ideas.

She bantered back and forth with the men, just enough to keep them interested. Always just enough. But not too much, Jake reminded himself. Once, in a fleeting moment, he had considered hiring a waitress, leaving his wife to stay home. He didn't quite like the men eyeing her, but at present, he was emptying a full cash register five and six times a day and the same at night, and the money looked damn good.

He sure didn't want to make any change that would hurt his business. Competition was bound to get heavier. His application for a beer license hadn't been approved. Some technicality about his building had screwed that up, so all he could really count on was a bonafide food business—and Grace. He swallowed his jealousy and decided to keep Grace on. Whenever he got a chance, he stopped in at Jhan's place ostensibly to have a beer, but at the same time, he counted the patrons eating there.

Jhan was doing record business over the bar and making a mint from his foreign food. There were an awful lot of Italians, Greeks, and practically any nationality you might name in town these days. It seemed they had to fill their guts at least once a day with spaghetti and meatballs or some other foreign concoction that Jake had never heard of.

Jake tried once to make spaghetti and meatballs, but every wop that ordered it stuck up his nose at the sauce and refused to eat the slop, as they called it. After that, Jake kept to his style of cooking.

Every businessman in town, including Jake, eyed the hotel with envy. Homer Gladrock, the present proprietor, was pleased with the deal he'd made with Jennie Boyd. Some of the businessmen in town wondered if he could have had an inkling somehow of this dam project. One of them came right out point-blank and asked him. Homer maintained he'd merely been a very fortunate recipient of good luck.

The hotel was certainly doing good business. Homer had applied for a liquor license as soon as he'd taken possession, and it had been granted promptly following an investigation. He hired a couple of women from a nearby village to do the cooking and chambermaid work. Both were in their early thirties and out to make a buck. Homer managed them nicely, and they in turn managed the dam workers that were in and out of the hotel. All told, it turned out to be a jolly as well as a profitable setup.

As the dam project became more fully launched, the hotel's clientèle became a mixture of salaried officials and migrant laborers. The hotel catered impartially to them all. It was rumored that every payday on the dam Homer would get $20,000 to $30,000 from the bank to make it convenient for the men to get their paychecks cashed right at the hotel. A good percentage of the checks was spent there, too. Marvin Dulle respected Homer's swift rise to a man of means and encouraged him to do business with him.

He let it be known in a casual manner about town that Homer held carte blanche status at the bank. Homer appreciated his sudden good standing with the bank, but remembered when it wasn't so good. He had to put up collateral much higher than the $200 loan warranted, so he did most of his business with out-of-town banks.

As Jake had guessed, competition did get heavier. Another diner sprang up, or so it seemed, overnight. Just out of town on a side road to the dam, the diner soon had its share of hungry men. Lea Jones, fat and jolly, knew how to prepare the kind of food that would stick to a man's ribs. She and her husband had been in this business most of their lives and followed one construction job after another. They had never accumulated a fortune, but this nomad existence suited them. Their fun-loving ways drew in as many customers as did their food.

On the whole, Gainesville was doing a rollicking business in just about anything you might name. Once the dam was completed, money would continue to flow as free as the B.W.S. expected the water to do.

The dam's wheel of progress was definitely hubbed by the town. Transient workers settled in and around it. They were accustomed to boom towns. They helped create them. Most of them had followed construction work of one type or another for the biggest share of their lives. They worked hard, played hard, and lived by the creed, "here today and gone tomorrow."

A few of the transients hauled in their living quarters. It was cheaper and more convenient to tow in their trailers than to muster up room and board in a new place. They were old hands at the business and knew as soon as the local people wised up, the prices of rooms and eats would go up, too.

At the request of the B.W.S., the town improvised a so-called trailer court in the back of the old Shaw building. A few scattered trees grew on the otherwise empty lot. The brook that crossed Main Street wound its gradually narrowing course along the back of the lot, separating it from a fairly large field that extended beyond the town's limits. Here and there under a shade tree, one might catch a glimpse of a dark blob, identifying an older trailer. Occasionally the sun bounced a beam against the bright aluminum of a new one, catching it back, reflecting a thousand multi-colored prisms.

Gene Mollen owned the handsome blue and silver trailer closest to the brook. He bought it new when he had decided to cast his lot in with the dam project. He'd never been in a trailer before, much less owned one. Gradually he was becoming used to being its owner and occupant. Somehow it seemed to add a bit of dignity to an otherwise rootless existence. Gene deplored the word "dignity." It wasn't dignity he wanted.

He only knew that some inner need, ever elusive, transitory at times, but always returning to gnaw away at his vitals, was satisfied to some extent by owning the trailer. Gene was baffled sometimes at his discontentment, and baffled, he drank more than his share of alcohol.

Gene was "in between women," as he termed it whenever he was devoid of female companionship. He lived alone in his trailer, pleasing himself by saying he neither wanted nor needed a woman. He accepted the fact that now and then he changed his mind. That's when he usually wound up at Maggie's establishment. He knew her place inside and out, had almost from the first night he had arrived in Gainesville. He couldn't in all honesty say that he enjoyed the company he met there, but on the other hand, the women were like the weave in an old carpet, worn but still usable. A man had to fulfill his basic needs.

Gene's determination to remain at his present job was strengthened by the last talk he had with his father. Both had parted in a fuming rage. Gene resolved to show him that he could make good without his damn political influence. Granted, he was the family black sheep, but he didn't intend to be a poor one.

He now owned construction equipment bought with the money he'd saved from his last job. Signing a contract with the B.W.S. had lifted his morale immensely. He figured his operational expenses were moderate, and by the time the dam was completed, he'd have a sizable bank account. This time he wasn't going to booze it too much, just enough to allay the boredom of this two-bit town.

Grace Hill became accustomed to having Gene patronize the restaurant. Some days he was in and out four or five times. She was used to the heavy familiarity that most of the dam workers assumed toward her and knew how to handle them. She didn't expect Gene to be any different the first time she saw him.

Somehow, right from the start, he had been set apart from the rest. He looked rough at times; that she couldn't deny. Somehow though, he impressed her as being different. He looked at her as long and as often as the other men, but it didn't have that calculating measure to it. He always sat where he knew she would be the one to wait on him, and his tips were more generous than the other men's.

Twice in the past week, he had passed her on the street on her way home and proffered her a ride. Each time, she had declined, still knowing that it would happen again, and one of these nights, she would accept. He knew Jake was still spending a good share of his free time either with some of the new floozies in town or at Maggie's.

Gene's evident interest was something she didn't want to combat.

WHEN GRACE LEAVES, EVERYTHING COLLAPSES

ON SUNDAY, JAKE'S restaurant could usually boast of having many customers.

But today had brought an unexpected lull and it was a welcome respite as far as Grace Hill was concerned. As usual, Jake griped if the place wasn't overflowing with eaters. He was hungover from the night before, and his head throbbed painfully. "Some business," he complained. "We've had exactly five customers this morning, and four of them for coffee or tomato juice. Must be everybody hung one on last night."

Grace sat at the counter, staring out the window, seeing and not minding how empty Main Street was.

"Don't-cha hear me talking to ya, woman? Speak up!" Jake shouted at her.

Grace pushed her coffee cup aside with her arm and turned on the stool to look at him. All of a sudden, it seemed her mind did a flip back. She didn't answer him, just stared, seeing a man that was more than commonly attractive. The firm, chiseled features belied his inherent weaknesses. Booze and women. A man who had handed out his filthy crap to her for almost ten years. A sneak, cheat, and just about anything one might name, she mentally tabulated.

She wondered what in the hell possessed her to have taken his bastardly treatment for so long. She didn't know, unless it was the fire-and-brimstone sermons preached from the pulpit, carrying the keynote of the narrow-mindedness in this stinking little town. She was afraid, but she finally decided. Fearful of a miserable little town whose morals were changing drastically every day, it had been slowly but surely evolving ever since the influx of dam workers.

Her thoughts jumbled, bringing Gene Mollen's image sharply to mind. Perhaps he wasn't as handsome as Jake. He was the rugged type, she reflected, gloatingly glad he was different. She had never intended to get involved as deeply as she was with Gene. True, she hadn't discouraged him when he had gone out of his way to pay her some little compliment in the restaurant, but neither had she figured on his becoming so vital to her that she'd throw discretion to the winds, time and again, to be with him.

She recalled with sheer ecstasy the nights she had allowed him to come to the house. Nights, she remembered revengefully, that Jake had passed pleasantly at Maggie's. She drew her breath in sharply, feeling again the sheer animal magnetism that drew her to Gene. He made love like a man possessed by the devil. She knew she couldn't hold out much longer against the wild feelings he stirred in her.

Suddenly, her unseeing stare was brought abruptly into focus. Jake slapped her. He slapped her hard, leaving an ugly red welt across her cheek. She steadied her position and put her hand on her face. "Who the hell you thinking about so much, you bitch, that you can't even hear when I talk to you?" Jake yelled.

"Thinking?" she questioned dazedly. Shockingly calm, she faced him. "That's all I've been doing these past few weeks. Not about other people, Jake, but about us!" Suddenly losing her dazed calmness, she screamed at him. "Us, Jake. You and me. Do you understand? I've thought of how you've cheated and lied while I've worked my ass off for you. Well, now I don't care anymore," she lashed out at him, "not even enough to fight with you."

"There's nothing, absolutely nothing so dead as a love that died aborning, and Jake, that's when you killed mine. You never stopped whoring around from the day I married you, and it looks like you never will. From now on, you can visit old Maggie's place without sneaking around. I'm leaving you and this damn town as well. And don't come looking for me," she screamed.

Her face became distorted with fury. An air of grim finality filled her voice. She gathered up her sweater and purse and opened the door. She let it bang shut behind her as she went out.

Jake, shocked into silence by the unexpected onslaught, looked at the palm of his hand. It still tingled from slapping her. Recovering his composure somewhat as a customer came in, he muttered angrily under his breath, "That little bitch, that stinking little bitch. She'll want to come back, and when she does, I won't have her."

Leaving the restaurant, Grace walked down Main Street, passing the Methodist church just as the bell tolled for morning services. Jake demanded her help in the restaurant on Sundays and during the rest of the week. She was more than thankful to have an excuse not to go. She nodded to a few acquaintances as they turned in at the church walk.

She paused momentarily to glance back at the couple who had just passed her. The man held the woman possessively by her arm. She seemed pale and hesitant, but he maneuvered her firmly through the church door and he seemed to have a long-suffering and self-righteous expression. Then again, maybe she saw herself in this woman she began to remember.

Sudden recognition flared in Grace's eyes. "My God!" she exclaimed. That's Fred Grimes and his wife. She didn't know either of them well, but she had once worked at a church supper with Sadie Grimes, the wife. She had seemed shy and withdrawn to the point of mousiness. Feeling sorry for her, Grace made a special effort to be friendly.

Mr. Grimes had also been at the supper, and Grace had instantly disliked him. Sitting across from the minister at the table, he had skillfully monopolized the conversation. Grace and the rest of the members knew why the minister practically fawned over him. Fred Grimes made the largest monetary contribution to the church yearly and made no bones about letting everyone know he did.

Shuddering, Grace walked on. She couldn't get Sadie's face out of her mind. The poor, poor woman, she commiserated. Him making her go in that church and face that bunch of damn do-gooders.

Just two weeks ago, Sadie had run off with one of the dam workers. She was such a quiet little thing that people couldn't believe it at first. Her husband finally located her. Accompanied by the minister, he went and brought her home. Grace wondered what brutality the two used to persuade Sadie to return. It hadn't been physical. Grace was sure of that—no bruises on the flesh that might be seen.

The minister would throw up his hands in horror at the mention of such treatment. No blows to the body would heal at that time. Only words. Words that pounded and accused, shriveling Sadie to a frightened, shamed piece of clay in their hands.

Revulsion washed over Grace as the minister stepped down from the church steps and laid a consoling hand on Mr. Grimes' arm. She pictured Sadie sitting in that church with her head bowed in shame. "Crucified, that's what she'll be." Not only by that sanctimonious husband of hers but by that bunch of hypocrites, calling themselves good Christians all the while.

Grace believed they'd not throw the first stone, but they'd take their 'pound of flesh' all the same.

She could almost hear their thoughts flitting back and forth among the pews. Any one of them could have said, "There but for the grace of God, go I," and shared a bit of Sadie's hell. None of them would. Instead, they'd lick their lips as they covertly watched her reaction to the minister's appropriate text on Jezebel. Grace sighed, thinking the poor thing would be better off in God's hell right now instead of being torn to bits by that bunch of masked vultures inside.

Giving herself a mental shake, Grace turned a corner, taking the street that led out of town toward the dam. At the edge of town, a car stopped beside her.

"Get in," Gene Mollen said, opening the car door.

Startled, Grace paused, then reluctantly got in beside him. "Guaranteed to keep tongues from wagging," she said cynically. Offering her a lighted cigarette, Gene half-smiled.

"Come on, out with it, honey. What's bothering you? I thought you were working today. What are you doing out this way?"

"Well, just don't sit here while people gape. Drive on up the road, and I'll tell you."

Gene drove on. He stopped on a side road two or three miles past the dam. "Alright, baby, we're away from prying eyes. Now tell me."

"To make it short, I fought with Jake and walked out on him."

"The sonofabitch hit you, didn't he?" Gene exploded. "Did he find out about us?"

"No, he doesn't know about us," Grace said, answering his last question. "He did slap me. He almost knocked me off the stool," she added. Hysteria edged her voice. "I'm only sure of one thing right now. I'm leaving him. I'm getting out of this town tonight," she said. "Take me home, please, Gene. I want to get packed and out before Jake comes home."

"Okay, honey," Gene comforted her, "but first promise me you'll call me at Jhan's when you're ready. I'll take you wherever you want to go. Promise?" he prodded. She nodded assent, and he backed the car out of the side road and headed back toward town.

"I'll call you in a couple of hours," Grace said, exiting the car in front of her house. "If you still want to take me, okay; if you don't, okay."

"I'll be ready and waiting, Sugar," Gene smiled.

Driving down the street, he whistled softly. "Cripes, I'm the guy that was through with women, and here I am sticking my neck out again," he thought. Making a wry face at himself in the rearview mirror, he said, "Gene, man, you're a number one sucker, but that gal's got it ready and waiting for you. What the hell is a man gonna do?"

Grace walked to the steps by her front door and entered the house, locking the door behind her. She moved restlessly about, touching this and that. She thought of Sadie Grimes being tortured in church by those hypocrites. She passed a hand over her aching brow.

"I feel like I'm standing on the edge of a precipice with a pack of wolves at my back," she said half-aloud. Moving across the room to the piano, she ran her fingers carelessly down the keyboard. The sudden discordant crash of notes jarred her out of her mental apathy. She snatched the wedding picture of her and Jake off the piano and flung it violently to the floor. She left it with the shattered glass bits all over the floor.

Time seemed to stop, slip into eternity or just disappear. Grace was unaware of it passing.

Trembling, she pulled her two suitcases out of the hall closet and crammed them full of her personal belongings. Snapping the locks, she carried them to the front porch. The phone rang. She lifted the receiver.

"Doll," Gene said, "it's ten minutes past the two hours you asked me to wait."

"I'm ready," she answered.

"Where to, honey?" Gene asked after she was settled in the car.

"Go over the 'Cat Hollow Road,'" she instructed. "It's a shortcut to the Manor. Surely you know that place, don't you?" she asked sweetly.

Gene grinned. "Grace, don't be naive, you know damn well I do," he admitted. "In fact," he continued, "every damn man that works in this valley has visited old Red's place in the Manor. There are plenty of buttered buns that hang out there. You can wine 'em, dine 'em, and take 'em upstairs for a buck two sixty."

"Nice place," Grace retorted. "Sounds like Maggie's dump."

The Cat Hollow Road was under construction. It was passable, though rutty and full of chuckholes.

"You'd think they'd fix this damn road," Grace said as she was bounced forward in the seat.

"They can't repair it yet," Gene protested. "The heavy equipment they're moving over it would tear it to pieces quickly." Just before the road terminated in the main highway, Gene gestured toward a field that, while escaping the roadside, was abruptly halted by a high ledge of rock a quarter mile away.

"See that steel framework rising at the base of that ledge, Grace? That's where the B.W.S. is sinking the No. 4 Shaft for the big tunnel. They started tunneling simultaneously here and at Shaft No. 1, just above Gainesville. At a given time, the two tunnels will join midway. Growing more enthused, he continued. "Honest Jed told me they won't be off-center a fraction of an inch when the two tunnels meet somewhere over in the mountains. Man, that takes brains to figure that out. Don't you think so, Grace?" he queried, catching her skeptical look.

"Really, Gene, I don't know," Grace replied. "Personally, I don't care if they tunnel through to China or to hell and back. All I care about right now is getting a job. I want to stop at Losingers Lodge on the other side of the Manor. I know they're hiring waitresses, and I just might get hired. If, however, you don't get going, I won't get there today."

"Suit yourself, sugar," Gene smiled as he pushed the accelerator almost to the floor.

Less than an hour later, Gene turned in at the lane that led to the resort. He braked the car to a stop in front of the main building.

"Now that I'm here, I'm scared to go in," Grace said as she smoothed her windblown hair back into place. "Movie stars and big shots from all over vacation here. Maybe I'm not the type they want in a place like this."

Gene squeezed her hand. "Honey, don't be a baby. Pull in your guts, stick out your chest," he grinned a little, "and walk right through that door as if you owned the place or one just like it. Go ahead," he urged as she hesitated.

"Unless you want to go back and take crap from Jake for the rest of your life. Well, there's another solution, for what it's worth, Grace," he added when she still didn't move. "You can come live with me in my trailer and you won't have to work."

Grace's face flamed scarlet.

"Get this straight, Gene, once and for all," she flared at him, "I'm not one of the two-bit whores you've known. I don't need you or anyone else to provide for me. I think I can manage to keep from starving—and I'm not afraid of work."

With eyes still flashing, she got out of the car and entered the main building.

"Man, what a spitfire!" Gene said.

A half-hour later, Grace emerged from the building. Back in the car, she couldn't keep the excitement out of her voice. "I landed a job, Gene," she exulted. "I'll work days with a break in the afternoon. Waitress, of course," she laughed, her irritation with him completely forgotten.

"Good girl," Gene commented. "How about a drink and dinner to celebrate? You know, woman, you made me forget all about eating, and if I wasn't such a handsome, steady, and easygoing good customer of Jhan's, he would have never let me in before hours this morning either. I'd have gone desert dry as well as hungry. Now what do the French say when a man gets in trouble? La Femme Fatale," he laughed.

"Gene, this is the first cordial I ever drank in my life." Seated across from him in the secluded restaurant, Grace lifted her glass mockingly. "Seems like you're a witness to 'my first time' in a number of things," she reflected.

Gene lifted his glass to hers. "I salute the gal who gets pensive on two martinis, a steak dinner, and a cordial she hasn't touched yet. Snap out of it, baby, we're going to celebrate when we finish here. Aren't we?" he asked as an afterthought.

"Gene, where did you learn French?" Grace asked.

"That is completely irrelevant right now. Gad! You buy a woman a drink and before you know it she wants to know when you cut your first tooth."

"Oh! Shut up, Gene," Grace came back at him. "Just stop trying to talk over my head. I had a year of French in school, and while it's probably as rusty as your guts, I still remember a bit of it. Breaking that phrase down you used a while back, what was it now?" She squiggled her nose delightfully. "Oh, yes, it was 'La Femme Fatale.' It means look for the woman when a man gets in trouble."

A flicker of surprise flashed over Gene's face.

"Honey," he said, "I'll get in trouble any time as long as you're at the bottom of it. You're sure as hell one hunk of a woman, with a body of a 'de Milo' and a brain as sharp as a rapier."

Grace lifted her glass in a mock toast.

"You're rather sharp yourself," she returned laughingly. Gene gazed at her.

They finished their drinks.

"Let's get out of here," Gene suggested, rising from the table. "I know a spot in Middleton where they have an orchestra and a cozy atmosphere. It's made to order for us."

"That's a bit too far," Grace protested. "I have to start my new job at ten tomorrow, remember?"

"It's no more than an hour, at most," Gene answered, fishing some change from his pocket and laying it on the table.

"I don't want to be any later than midnight getting back to the hotel. I don't want to make a bad impression right at the start," Grace cautioned him.

"It's too bad you didn't tell them you wouldn't be using the room until tomorrow night," Gene commented.

"Don't get any ideas, Gene. I get my room and board—and salary. I intend to use all three. Starting tonight."

"Did I tell you I think you're cute?" Gene's amused smile flashed as he started the car.

Conversation took a turn as Gene drove fast but skillfully through the traffic. Grace seemed preoccupied with her thoughts. They had passed through several small villages and were nearing the outskirts of the city when Gene spoke up.

"Powder your nose, honey. We're practically there." Grace dutifully opened her purse and took out her compact. "I was only kidding, you little goon," Gene laughed.

"Nonetheless, it's good advice," Grace answered as she wiped the powder puff over her nose.

Gene drove through what was apparently the center of the city and turned into a side street. He swerved the car into the curb, parking it expertly in front of a stone-faced hotel.

"Here we are, sweetheart," he said, opening her door. "It took us exactly fifty-five minutes. Now, how's that for driving." There was a hint of pride in his voice.

"You'll do," Grace giggled as she submitted to his helping hand. "I don't know yet if it's you or the drinks that make me feel so heady. But Gene, I've decided all I want is my own back right now."

The string orchestra was playing in harmony as they entered.

LET GO OF HER, LOSE EVERYTHING

THE STUDENT NURSES entered the classroom. Becky Hawk was among them.

A few minutes later, Mrs. Norma Stanley, the director of nurses, arrived. Stern but pleasant, she was as well-liked by the student body as well as by the nursing school faculty.

"Get your wraps," she announced quietly to the assemblage of students. "They are holding an autopsy at the morgue this morning, and we are going to participate."

Becky walked with Aldeen Stewart as the class filed out. "This is the last one, Becky," remarked Aldeen on their way to the morgue.

"Yes, this is the twelfth and completes our 'post mortems,'" Becky confirmed.

"We couldn't do any more before we leave for New York, even if we weren't on the twelfth," Aldeen added. "These years have passed quickly, haven't they, Becky?" she continued, straying from the present subject. "Five more days and we start our affiliation in Bellevue."

"Wonder who the sawbones will be morning?" Becky pondered, switching the conversation back to the post mortem subject.

"Probably Dr. Bentley, with you as assistant as usual," Aldeen supplied. "How come, Becky?" she questioned impulsively. "You didn't strike me as being the brilliant type when you first came here."

Becky opened her mouth to speak, but was cut off again immediately by Aldeen.

"Oh, we all know you study hard. In fact, you've turned into a regular bookworm. Guess that accounts for your high rating, but you've changed so much in other ways, too. You never have time for fun anymore. All you think or talk about is blood and guts," Aldeen finished disgustedly.

"I know you detest autopsies, Aldeen, but why rant off at me?" Becky exploded. "Sure, I'm a bookworm if that's what you wish to call it. I have to study simply because I, or no one else, can grasp everything just from the lectures the doctors give. In fact," she continued half resentfully, "you could do with a little more studying yourself. Your grades aren't exactly the best, you know."

"Just to keep the record straight, Hawk, I expect to graduate though," Aldeen retorted. "I don't intend to be a personified collection of noble ideas or a replica of Florence Nightingale, but I'll make it, and I won't miss all the fun while I'm doing it either."

She paused a minute and continued in the wake of Becky's silence.

"You're much too clinically minded, Hawk. If someone mentions the word 'body' to you, you start looking around for something dead or think of it as reposing on a marble slab in the morgue, or to that effect," she added.

"You'll wish you'd taken anatomy more seriously, Aldeen, when we get to Bellevue," Becky told her.

"Anatomy be damned. When the good-looking interns in Bellevue start looking around for a body, they're going to find mine," Aldeen joked, "and it won't be a dead one either."

"Think and do as you will," Becky replied angrily, "but I happen to want more out of life than just fun. I was born in poverty and grew up with it all around," she continued passionately, "and I'm sick to death of it. I intend to be somebody, not just a body. That's what my parents wanted for me and that's how it's going to be."

"You know, Aldeen, I may have had hayseed in my hair two years ago, as you often insisted I had, but I think I've washed most of it out. But you, you had the stamp of spoiled brat then and you still have it.

I don't think you'll ever outgrow it." Becky stalked angrily through the morgue's door.

Aldeen laid her hand over Becky's as they took their seat in the morgue amphitheater. "I'm sorry, Hawk," she whispered. "I think I'm just jealous. Please don't be angry." Catching the annoyed expression on Mrs. Stanley's face at their obvious inattention, Becky refrained from answering.

Dr. Bentley entered, pulling the sheet off the body lying on the steel table in the morgue center.

"Today," he announced cheerfully, "we're going to probe the brain. I contend this man had a malignant tumor recessed deeply in the medulla oblongata. X-rays didn't show it, so my colleagues," he paused a moment to cast a humorous eye at three doctors sitting on the benches to his left, "say it isn't there. We shall see," he said.

"Miss Hawk, may I have your assistance, please?"

Squirming inside, knowing exactly what Aldeen and the rest of the class were thinking, Becky left her seat to stand at the head of the morgue table with Dr. Bentley.

"No wonder she's so smart," Aldeen whispered to the girl beside her. "Old Bentley always asks for her when he has something intricate to perform."

"I think he likes bodies, especially Hawk's," the other girl returned maliciously.

The autopsy later confirmed Dr. Bentley's diagnosis and the class was excused for lunch. "He's the greatest," Becky stated admiringly, her altercation with Aldeen forgotten.

"Sorry, I can't seem to get enthused," Aldeen replied flippantly. "By the way," she asked blandly, "can you guess what's on the menu for lunch?"

"Not hash and strawberry Jello!" Becky protested.

"Right!" Aldeen assured her. "They always serve that on the day we have an autopsy. I think they grind up the organs and congeal the blood."

Becky gagged. "I'm not going to lunch, Aldeen. I have something I want to finish in the classroom."

"So be it," Aldeen laughed, going into the cafeteria.

The last day before the students were to leave for their affiliation in New York City, they were summoned together for final instructions on behavior befitting almost-graduate nurses. Mrs. Stanley addressed the group in words of severity, tempered with affection.

Upon concluding her speech, she admonished, "Remember, you, as an individual or collectively as a student body, represent this hospital training school. Your work, appearance, or conduct is a mirrored reflection of our teaching. We are expecting the best from you. All classes have been canceled for the remainder of the day, and you are free to do as you choose. However, at this time I'd like to make an announcement," she smiled broadly.

"The teaching staff has arranged a small tea party over in the club room in honor of your departure tomorrow. We'd be honored if you would join us."

"This damn regimentation has practically killed me all through training," Aldeen complained to Becky on their way to the room.

"Well, attending this tea party isn't mandatory," Becky retorted.

"Maybe not in so many words," Aldeen griped, "but just try to get out of it."

The next day on their way to New York City, Aldeen said, "Everything passes."

"Are you referring to cars?" Becky joked as their bus driver maneuvered the bus they were in slowly along Route 17.

"Well, not specifically, just everything in general," Aldeen replied.

"Since when did you turn to philosophy?" Becky rejoined impudently.

"I was merely comforting myself with trite sayings as I thought of the next nine months in the Bellevue labor camp," Aldeen explained dejectedly.

"Well, cheer up 'fun gal,' there have been many that walked before us."

"Oh, nuts!" was all Aldeen said in response.

Once the affiliating students were absorbed in and adjusted to the huge hospital's well-oiled routine, time passed quickly for many of them. Where most of their studying had been confined to the theoretical in their previous nursing program, it was now applied and demonstrated in a practical manner.

Becky discovered the change to be exciting and challenging. Aldeen simply discovered the interns, and they discovered her, with young Dr. Giles completing his second year of interning, superseding the others.

Becky's class rating climbed from above average to excellent. Aldeen's remained at a passing, but mediocre grade. Both girls enjoyed their new environment, each for a different reason, as the the nine-month affiliation melted away.

Becky threw down a thesis she was working on to gaze at Aldeen lazily lounging in a chair. The calendar showed two weeks remaining. "What did you say, Aldeen?" she questioned.

"I just invited you to dinner with Dr. Giles and me tonight," Aldeen repeated.

"Dinner!" Becky exclaimed. "You're on the three-to-midnight shift tonight. How can you go out to dinner? I'd like to know."

"It was supposed to be my night to work," Aldeen conceded, "but I switched with one of the other students and the supervisor OK'd it. Becky," she continued hesitantly but determinedly, "I want to tell you something, but you have to promise not to breathe a word."

"Where's the body?" Becky teased, "I'll help dispose of it."

"This is serious," Aldeen protested solemnly.

"OK, I promise. Now get it off your chest," Becky suggested.

Aldeen rose from the chair and walked over to the window, gazing down at the streaming traffic on the busy street. After a moment, with her back still toward Becky, she announced suddenly, "I'm getting married tonight."

"To whom?"

"Gerry. Dr. Giles, that is," Aldeen replied. "Surely, you know we've been seeing a great deal of each other. Even if it is against the rules, we managed."

"But what about your other weeks of affiliation?" Becky asked quietly.

"We're keeping it quiet. I'm going to finish the course and by then he'll have finished his internship," Aldeen said, but had a triumphant glow about her as she turned to face Becky.

"We're going to India. Gerry has a missionary brother there, and we'll both be working in the same locality, only ours will be the medical field.

Can you imagine me standing the trials and tribulations as a struggling young doctor's wife in such primitive surroundings?"

"Are you sure this is what you want?" Becky asked her.

"I love him," Aldeen answered softly, "and he wants to do research in India, so it's okay by me. If he wanted to take off for the moon, I'd feel the same way. And Becky," Aldeen continued, "I'd like you to know I have been wrong about a number of things. Until I started dating Gerry, I was that spoiled brat you called me once, but I've changed. Enough, at least, that I can think of other people's feelings as well as my own. I want you to be my witness tonight."

"Well, I can't say I approve of the chances you're both taking of being discovered and kicked out before you've completed, but of course I'll come along," Becky assured Aldeen. "You're almost family," she added, hugging Aldeen.

"We must leave here by six o'clock," Aldeen emphasized. "We've made all the arrangements in Matamoras, Pennsylvania, with a justice of the peace. He assured us that the announcement won't be in the New York papers, so we're reasonably safe on that score."

"I'll be ready and waiting," Becky assured her. "Now, if I have to squander away my evening with you, I've got to get on with this thesis. I'm going over to the library, but I'll be back by five at least. By the way, who's standing up with Gerry?"

"The JP's brother," Aldeen answered. "We just don't want any more in on it than we have to have. Gerry did give in to me about you though. Not even my parents know about it. Simple and quick with no fuss."

"Okay, I'll be back soon," Becky said, closing the door.

Later that evening they got together for the clandestine knot-tying.

"Well, that's over with, honey. At least I've made an honest woman out of you," Gerry Giles laughed nervously as the three of them jumped into a car after the short marriage ceremony.

"Gerry, what an awful thing to say," Aldeen reproved him, "and especially in front of Becky."

"Sorry, I wasn't thinking how it sounded," Gerry apologized. "Let's wait until we get back to the city to have dinner, shall we?" he suggested.

"No," Aldeen refused. "I want to eat and have a drink right here in this town. I really think I need two highballs right now."

"Well, I guess I married an alcoholic," Gerry laughed. "How about you, Becky? Want a drink now?" he asked.

"Anything you two decide is okay by me," Becky replied. "It's your honeymoon," she teased.

It was close to midnight when Dr. Giles stopped the car halfway up the block from the hospital. Becky almost dropped her purse in surprise when Aldeen followed her out.

"It can wait," Aldeen replied to her questioning stare. "Gerry and I both have to be on the job at seven in the morning." A silence fell between the two girls as they readied for bed a half hour later.

"She seems happy and yet she doesn't," Becky thought, reviewing the night's events. It was toward early morning when Becky was startled out of a deep sleep by the sound of Aldeen's muffled crying in the next bed. "I just knew it," she thought. "The portent of this quick marriage isn't as good as it should be." Sensing it wasn't the time to let Aldeen know she was awake, Becky just lay still, thinking.

The affiliating period came to a close, and the students returned to their training school. Aldeen acquired a tense look foreign to her usual happy-go-lucky manner. Her associates, with Becky excepted, attributed it to the pressure of waiting out the next six weeks before the students could take the state board exams to obtain licenses.

Many times, Becky gazed at Aldeen, but refrained from being inquisitive. They made the trip together to New York City for their state exams. Three tense, grueling days of it finally ended, and they returned to Whorton to await the results.

Becky and Aldeen sat in the nurse's recreation room. The radio played softly. Aldeen sat idly flipping the pages of a magazine.

"These last three years went awfully fast, now that I've had time to think about it, don't you think so?" Becky said to Aldeen, hoping to start a conversation.

"All but these last three months," Aldeen affirmed.

"I suppose they did go slowly for you," Becky conceded, "but it must have been the same for Gerry, don't you think?"

"Of course," Aldeen admitted, "but the waiting is just about over. As soon as I get my exam report from the state board, I'm leaving for New York City."

"You two were very, very lucky that you didn't get found out."

"Becky, we haven't spent one night together since we were married. Admittedly, I saw him for a few hours when we were in the city taking exams. It's been hell," Aldeen said quietly, "but it will soon be water over the dam."

Aldeen's words brought a momentary shiver down Becky's spine. That dam, home, memories, her parents gone and never having seen her accomplishment.

"Let's go bowling, Aldeen," she suggested. "I'm tired of just sitting here." She rose from the chair and stretched luxuriously.

"I don't dare," Aldeen refused, then paused in confusion while a slight pink mantled her face. "Well, what I mean is," she rattled on, "that I have some things I want to do in my room."

"I think I will anyways," Becky answered as if she hadn't noted something amiss.

The next day brought the anxiously awaited exam grades from the state board. Aldeen glanced at hers and proffered it to Becky.

"Why, you're only three points less than me," Becky exclaimed in astonishment. "How did you ever do it?"

"I had a goal to reach, remember?" Aldeen smiled.

"Yes, Mrs. Dr. Giles," Becky replied.

Three weeks later, Becky stood on a Long Island pier with Aldeen's parents. They watched as Aldeen and Gerry walked up the gangplank to stand on the ship's deck, waving until they were but a blob in the distance.

Becky glanced at Aldeen's parents, wondering how much they knew. Nothing, she decided, taking in their happy faces, saddened only by the knowledge that their only child would be living oceans away from them.

Refusing their invitation to dinner, Becky bid them goodbye. She hailed a cab and to the driver's question, "Where to?"

She directed him to Bellevue. Arriving, she entered the familiar building, walked into the director's office, applied for and a week later got the position as second charge nurse of the surgical ward.

FLIRT. FIGHT. FALL. REPEAT

WINTER IN GAINSVILLE brought work on the dam to a standstill.

Snow covered the havoc wrought by the project. Where it once hung caressingly on tree branches, snow now made an incongruous pattern of monumental drifts where the trees once stood. Strong winds howled over it all, lashing out in fury at its clear sweep over the dam sector.

One would have thought the town would have frozen to immobility, but it didn't. It was hot as hell and still heating up. Time hung heavy on its inhabitants. The men were laid off from work until spring, but their unemployment checks were ready and waiting each week.

The town was held in the throes of one big hangover. The men boozed it up, and their women, deciding that what was "sauce for the gander was sauce for the goose," did likewise.

Only a few of the smarter businessmen tended to business. Jake wasn't one of them, though his restaurant business was still a profitable one. Grace was no longer there to flirt with his male customers, but the men still had to eat. As one man bluntly said to Jake, "Now we get a charge out of coming here instead of a raise." Jake had all-male help.

Grace had served him with a divorce summons four months earlier. He hadn't been forced to appear in court to answer it, so he had let it ride. He was, at present, devoid of marital ties and had mentally kicked himself in the ass a dozen times because of it. He should have prevented Grace from walking out on him somehow, he thought. He never dreamed she'd leave him for good, but the little bitch had, it seemed, and he missed her.

He now stood behind the counter, wiping it down.

"Hey, Jake," called out Jess, eating at the far end of the counter.

"Coming right up," Jake answered, drawing a cup of coffee.

"You going down to the flats tonight?" Jess asked as Jake paused in front of him. "Hennesey's got his liquor license, you know."

"Is that right?" Jake sounded somewhat surprised.

"Yep," Jess continued, "he's having his grand opening tonight, hillbilly band and all the trimmings."

Jake reflected for a minute. "Might be fun at that," he finally admitted.

"You old son of a bitch, it's about time you got away from Maggie's," laughed Jess. "You'll wear yourself to a frazzle in that old bag's harem. There ain't a good wiggle left in the whole damn bunch of 'em."

"Well, you ought to know," Jake shot back. "Let me see, I've seen you up there three times so far this week."

"Oh, hell, Jake!" coaxed Jess, pushing the remark to one side. "Come on down with me tonight. There's new stuff floating in from all over. We'll have ourselves a ball, man!"

"Well, guess my counterman could handle the trade alone for a few hours," Jake consented. "And if all that new stuff is floating around as you say, Jess, we'll have to bring some of it down. I sure haven't been getting in anything new lately except a rut."

"Not even a rut, Jake," Jess said, getting up from the stool. "All old Maggie has up there is holes. Be ready at ten," he advised Jake as he left the restaurant.

The Hennesey Hotel was ablaze with lights. It was nearing eleven o'clock, and the place was jam-packed. Mr. Hennesey stood by the doorway between the bar and the dining room, as he called it. His gaze traveled admiringly over his menage. He had long called his place a hotel, but tonight was the first he'd considered it a paying one.

He couldn't complain, really. He'd managed to make a living over the years, putting up fishermen and hunters from the city during their seasons for the sports.

His biggest windfall came last year when a group of politicians, nine in all, came from Buffalo for the deer season. They brought their wives along too—or at least that's how they registered. Mr. Hennesey thought they seemed unusually amorous for married couples, but after all, it wasn't any of his business. He charged them an unusually high rate for their rooms, but nobody squawked.

They even managed a hundred-dollar tip among them for Mr. Hennesey when they left. All told, he made a darn good profit. He also knew how to keep his big Irish mouth shut so he'd have their patronage next year.

In the meantime, he had managed to build an addition to the hotel. Made from hewn logs, one story high, it gave the rest of the frame building a look of rustic charm. He had arranged tables up and down both sides of the room and added an old piano to the corner.

There was plenty of space left in the center for square dancing. Six sets of dancers were whooping it up as he stood there looking around. The women squealed in delighted protest as the square dance caller yelled out, "Swing your partners," and their partners swung them high in the air.

Mr. Hennesey kept a watchful eye over it all. Some of the people he knew, some he didn't. He didn't quite place the couple at the third table on the left when they had first come in and had gotten a momentary start when he went over to serve them.

"Hi, Mr. Hennesey," Grace Hill and Gene Mollen said simultaneously. Then they laughed and hooked their pinkies together. Gene looked up.

"Hennesey," he said, "this woman is a witch. A charming one to be sure," he amended.

"No, you're not supposed to talk," Grace protested, "until after we've made a wish. Now it won't come true."

Mr. Hennesey smiled, all the time thinking what a helluva nerve Grace had to come back in the vicinity of her hometown after walking out on Jake like she had, especially with another man. He remembered them all right.

He took their order and walked back to the barroom. He almost dropped his tray of glasses when he saw who was standing at the other end of the bar. "There's the makings of a fight here tonight," he said quietly to the bartender, giving him his order. "That's Jake Hill who just came in, and it's his wife sitting out there in the other room with Gene Mollen. Keep an eye out for trouble, you hear?" The bartender raised his hand in an okay gesture.

"Make it a couple of boilermakers, Bud," Jess ordered the bartender. "Jake and me have got a little dancin' to do out there in a few minutes. Better make it four," he retracted as two girls edged up closer to him and Jake.

"What's workin', babe, you two lonesome?" Jake asked, moving over to give them more standing room.

"Well, now we're alone but not too lonesome," the redhead drawled, standing closer to Jake. "We could, however, stand the company of the two best-looking men here."

"Guess me and Jess can fix you girls up, can't we, Jess?"

Both men smirked as the bartender set their drinks in front of them.

"I'm Marjorie, and this is Lena," the redhead introduced.

"Jess and Jake," Jake reciprocated with an expansive smile.

"Dance?" he invited as the hillbilly band sent forth the appealing strains of "Redwing" for the evening's first-round dance number. Jake pushed the way through the crowd to the dance floor. He felt the soft curve of her breast as she melted tightly against him. His breath came hot on her cheek as he pulled her even closer.

"Look at that whore master," Grace said to Gene, gesturing slightly toward the dancers.

"Who, honey?" Gene whispered. He couldn't single out whom she meant at first among the gyrating couples.

"Oh," was all he said when he finally saw Jake and his girl, but his face suddenly became bleak.

"To us." Grace lifted her glass to Gene's. Her eyes sparkled as she looked at him.

"Princess, I believe you really mean it."

"I do, Gene. I couldn't care less about him. My divorce is final, and I'm free as a bird. He didn't even appear to contest the divorce, as you know. It's over and done with between us, so stop looking so gloomy."

Gene stared at her hard for a couple of seconds. "Grace, there are a few things I haven't told you. I probably wouldn't now, but you're so darn honest with me that I think I owe it to you. I'm not married, as you believe. True, I was. But I've been divorced for six years. My ex-wife has custody of our only child. A boy. He's eight years old now. I never see either of them. The boy's mother makes it too difficult. Maybe it's better this way."

He paused for a moment and then continued.

"I had to marry her, Grace. We weren't really in love, but we had an affair while we were both getting settled in college. Neither of us had been completely on our own before. We had too much money, too much freedom, and when it came right down to it, no brains. I can't blame either one of us too much. It was just one of those things. My old man wouldn't hear of any alternative except marriage. Our families were friends for years, and to both sides, marriage was the only solution."

"We quit college and tried to make the marriage work, but somehow it just wasn't in the cards. A year after our son was born, his mother divorced me, and I joined the Air Force."

"I couldn't see eye to eye with my old man when I got out of the service, so I started roaming the country, finally winding up in this business, and I like it. Honey, this is the sum and substance of Gene Mollen, period!"

Reaching across the table, Grace grasped his hand. "I love you, Gene," she whispered. His eyes caressed her as he whispered, "Baby, let's get out of here. I don't like the way Jake keeps eyeing us. First thing we know, we'll be having trouble with him."

Getting up from the table, he held her arm as he guided her out of the building.

Jake's bloodshot eyes grew redder as he noted their departure.

"You with me or against me?" Marjorie asked, moving her hot lips sensuously against his throat.

"Against you, baby! Just like I wanna be, only closer," Jake answered, jerking her hard up against him. "How about you?" She let him feel the full length of her body against his, soft and yielding, in lieu of answering.

Opening the car door, Gene helped Grace in, slipping his hands under her buttocks. He slid her over to almost under the steering wheel. Getting in from the other side, he pulled her into his embrace. With one hand cupping her breast, his lips moved slowly over hers, eliciting little moans of rapture from her as his tongue darted in and out between her lips.

"Honey, oh baby, I've got to have you," he panted. "Tonight, I can't wait any longer."

"Please, Gene, not here," Grace protested over her own ecstatic response.

"There's a place down the river then," Gene said, releasing her and starting the motor. "It's just below East Branch," he added. "It has a small bar and rooms available upstairs. The owner and his wife separated a few weeks ago, and he's out to make a fast buck without too many questions. Now, honey, I've never taken a woman there if that's what you think," he said in answer to her stricken look.

"I've drunk there, though, many a night with the owner, both of us drowning our troubles, as it were."

"Here we are," Gene smiled happily, stopping the car a short time later in the parking area in front of a yellow small-framed building.

"Why, I've been by here oodles of times," Grace exclaimed. "I've never been inside, but supposing he recognizes me from the restaurant?"

"He won't," Gene reassured her, "for the simple reason that he doesn't know anyone around here that well. He bought this place after the dam was started. The former owners left for California before you even left here."

The bar was deserted except for the owner, who sat rather dejectedly behind the bar. "How you doing, Gene?" he asked, giving Grace a quick look.

"Fine, Mac. How about mixing us a couple of highballs?"

Grace went to the ladies' room, and the bartender set the drinks on the bar.

"I'd like a room for the night," Gene said bluntly after Grace was out of earshot. "For two of us," he emphasized.

"Take your pick," the owner said. "So far, I'm empty. Don't know what it'll be like after Hennesey's closes tonight, though. If you want it kept private, take the room at the head of the stairs. First one to the left. Just let me know when you're ready to leave in the morning, and I'll give you the all-clear signal."

Gene slipped him a ten-dollar bill and paid for the drinks when Grace came back.

"Come on, honey," Gene urged. Grace finished her drink and followed him upstairs.

"Gene, you hurried me too much. I've got to have a cup of coffee. Do you suppose they have any downstairs?" Grace asked.

"Well, I'll go see," Gene offered. "You're not sick, are you?" he questioned, with his hand on the doorknob. She grinned and stuck out her tongue at him.

"Nope," she teased. "I just want some coffee."

As soon as Gene closed the door behind him, she pulled off her clothes, ran her hand smoothly over her naked curves, and tumbled into the bed.

Gene had another drink while he waited for the coffee.

"How about shooting a game of craps after you take this up?" the owner invited Gene, setting the coffee in front of him.

"Can't," Gene smirked, "I've got things to do."

"Oh, hell," the owner griped. "Go up and sink your anchor once and come on back for a while. It's early yet," he protested.

"Ask me again, say, in two or three days," Gene laughingly replied on his way upstairs.

It was after 4 a.m. when Jess let Jake out of the car in front of his house.

"Bet Jake will be looking that redhead up again just as soon as he gets over tonight," Jess chuckled to himself. "Cripes, he walks like he'd been riding a bucking bronco."

STACK THE STONES AND BURY THE BONES

'HONEST' JED BARNES returned to Gainesville.

He had left behind him the essence of New York's culture, a culture that had lulled and bored him through the winter months. He had a primeval need for Gainesville or its counterpart. Here, in the town, directing the dam project, he was an entity, part and parcel of the town, fulfilling a need for progress and unwittingly satisfying one of his own.

He was 'Honest Jed,' dressed like an ordinary laborer when he was on the job, enjoying the smell of sweat on himself and the dank earth under his feet.

Spring was early, but undeniable. Robins heralded its arrival while Jed breathed deeply of its freshness. The first morning after his arrival, he didn't bother to take his car out of the hotel garage, deciding instead to walk over to the dam sector. The old riverbed lay drying under the blue April skies.

"It's ready and waiting for me to begin," Jed thought as he jumped across a boggy spot. He felt a sharp sting on his ankle as he landed on a fragment of a burial urn with the name "Hawk" on it. He felt the warm, sticky feel of blood as he reached down and touched it.

"Cripes, I should have known better," he cursed as he picked up a jagged piece of broken urn. It was shattered when young Becky dropped her parent's cremated remains a few years earlier from a plane piloted by Gene Mollen.

"If I had worn my engineer boots like any fool would, this couldn't have happened."

He wrapped his handkerchief tightly over the wound. He brought a piece of the broken fragment - the name on crumbling as he held it - old Doc's office.

"It isn't deep," Doc announced, treating and bandaging the jagged cut on Jed's ankle. "I'll have to give you a shot to combat infection, though," he added.

In this irony, Doc, who attended to the dead this urn contained and who helped guide Becky in that troubled time to support the cremation, was now yet again and unknowingly touched by that event.

It seems that in Gainsville much never goes away, the past recirculates into the present, taking on another form or some fragment finds its way back into the circular pattern of life there. Unbroken patterns of behavior - womanizing, boozing, exploiting, swindling and other kinds of decadence - become incorporated in a circle of life and death.

"Well, in my work, I've learned it's wise to let the doctor see the source of the trouble if possible," Jed laughed. "Guess that must be a piece of old Indian pottery," he commented. "I found a couple of arrowheads along there last fall, too. Must be the Indians used that old riverbed for a burial spot by the looks of things over there."

"Umm, it could be," Doc admitted, but in his mind, he simply couldn't associate that broken piece of pottery with Indians of a hundred years past. Yet somehow, there was something about it that nagged his memory for recognition.

He threw it in his wastebasket. He couldn't be bothered with trivia, he decided as he gave Jed a shot of penicillin in his rear.

Jed hobbled about the town and the dam area the following week, preparing the essentials for restarting the dam construction. Carmen arrived within the week. Crews were rehired, and the town once again responded to alarm clocks as the men became part of the dam sector panorama.

Jed Barnes had engineered the channeling and re-channeling of many waters. Under his orders, Carmen directed the clearing of the river's former bottom to make way for the starting point of the dam's retaining wall. The clearing of the old riverbed was facilitated by the use of gas shovels.

The huge shovels scooped up muck and debris and emptied them into the cavernous holding containers as they lined up to commence and complete their endless cycle of taking their loads to a designated spot, emptying them, and then returning to reload.

The work progressed with a nameless rhythm, without incident, except on one occasion that gave Jed a bad feeling. He was walking slowly along the old riverbank, pausing a moment to watch a gas shovel at work. Suddenly, the shovel operator yelled, "Alert!" Every man, including Jed, froze in his tracks.

The operator swerved the shovel's gaping jaw high in the air, dropping it down swiftly within a couple of feet of Jed and scooped up a shovel of dirt with a coiled rattler atop.

Now, yelling a warning, he maneuvered the shovel's steel jaws, dropping the dirt and snake as far as possible from Jed and the men below. The operator covered the few feet of ground, separating Jed from the rattler in a couple of seconds, then killed it instantly with the shovel. The snake measured a little under five feet in length and sported six buttons on its tail.

Jed never flicked an eyelash at his close call. He continued on with his work after warning the men to be careful. In time, measured by the engineers' chronology, the clearing of the two hundred feet of riverbed hadn't taken long. It was now ready for the laying of the retaining wall, or more technically described as a core wall, to be constructed across its width.

Jed handpicked a sure-footed and nimble crew to lay the core wall under Carmen's orders. He knew from experience that before its completion, the project's death toll would rise by at least one or two. It was dangerous work, presenting many hazards. A moment of unawareness, and a man could come face to face with his Maker. Every precaution was taken to keep accidents down, but still, they happened.

The basic work began. Carmen was edgy and sharp with his tongue. The crew worked methodically. Jed was all over the dam sector, but could be found more often near the core wall construction. He checked the sixty-foot caissons as they were forced through the earth to be embedded, sometimes ninety feet down, in a bed of solid rock. These were the core wall footings, and Jed checked and double-checked before he'd approve Carmen's reports.

Supported by huge abutments, a network of concrete and steel rose gradually and gracefully out of the old riverbed, the steel piling pointing implacably toward the sky. Thirty feet wide at ground level, the massive frame narrowed as it ascended until it reached a bare four feet across the top or 'cat-walk' as the crew called it. Sixty feet high, spanning the riverbed and a goodly distance on each side, the core wall could have been judged, not too inaccurately, a good half mile long.

Constantly packing the dirt down at the core wall's base were the 'gandy' operators. Honest Jed always got a kick out of watching them maneuver their gandy machines. The gandys weren't large. One measured, possibly three feet high, cylindrically shaped, with a center mobile shaft attached to a top handle and a bottom disc. They were rather tricky to handle.

It wavered a man's grip when the compression-fired shaft was forced violently up in the cylinder to drop with a thud when the spring was released, tamping the earth down with its heavy disc.

But Rod Shaver and Bill Decker, his brother-in-law, were two of the few workers who could operate their gandys expertly. Bud was forever mimicking something or someone with his gandy. He'd shimmy with it, let his grip loosen enough so it would head toward Bill, who worked beside him, and raise hell in general whenever the foreman had his back turned. If it weren't Bud clowning around, it was Bill.

They said their foreman was just a shit head, brainwashed by the engineers, and laughed at the other gandy shakers for their timidity when he was around.

On one occasion, Jed happened to be on the 'cat-walk,' completely unnoticed by the gandy shakers below. The foreman had gone into town to get something for Carmen, and the men started goofing off. Bud had a harmonica clamped between his teeth and both hands tight on his gandy. Moving his tongue over it, he started playing "Turkey in the Straw." Bill and two of the other gandy shakers, taking Bud's cue, started a regular hoe-down using their gandys as partners. Bill had just called out, "Swing your partners," when Jed called down.

"You damn hillbillies down there, get to work. If you want to fiddle or diddle, get your pink slips and go on up to Maggie's."

Bud laughed, and so did Bill. Both of them knew Jed wouldn't fire either of them. They knew it as well as Jed did himself. The four men started their gandys to tamping the earth down again. Jed walked away, smiling to himself as he descended the core-wall. He liked most of the local people, but he especially liked Bud and Bill. He liked their work, but most of all, he liked their irrepressible laughter and down-to-earth honesty.

He admired the way he'd seen Bud raise a guy two inches in the air with a swift uppercut from his right and sprawl him six feet across a barroom floor. Jed had seen Bud smile just as he hit the loud-mouthed troublemaker. But Jed noticed his eyes had been as hard as agate. Jed liked a man who could smile when he was killing mad. He was like that himself.

The summer days waxed long and hot as the core-wall frame neared completion. The seemingly endless heat engulfed the laborers. Steel piling glutted the sun of its infrared rays and cast its surfeit over the men unmercifully.

It was midnight. The crew had put in a hard day's work. Welding and bolting high on the 'catwalk' was nerve-wracking, as well as a high-paying job. Tempers were short at the end of the day, especially today. Carmen and Jed had been inspecting every minute detail as the men worked.

"There's absolutely no room for errors," Jed explained patiently, but firmly to the men as he made one of them recheck a bolt that had already been tightened to its full capacity.

"Keep that pisspot on your head where it belongs," Jed warned another. "You want one of them red-hot rivets through that thick skull of yours?"

The worker grinned disarmingly as the sparks showered above him from the riveter's gun. "Okay, Boss." He put the steel helmet back on his head and swore a blue streak as Jed went on.

The day had been a weary one, not only for the laborers but for the top-level men as well.

"Bet them bastards will tank up tonight," Jed commented as the crew clocked in their time at the end of the day.

"Can't blame them," Carmen answered tersely.

Four of the 'cat-walkers' now were sitting at Jhan's Bar. Beer hadn't been potent enough to loosen the tension in their taut muscles, so they had switched to liquor.

"Hey, Jhan," one of them called, "let's give with the bar dice, huh?"

"Now, boys," Jhan said, "you know I don't allow bar dice in here. The B.W.S. cops are breathing down my neck now."

"Well, you goddamn Lithuanian, somebody oughta breathe down it with a little water," Lou returned. "You're greasy, your place is greasy, and for two cents I'd clean you both up."

Glaring menacingly at Jhan, he slid off the bar stool. The other three got up, too.

"C'mon Lou, let's get outta this dump," Lou's buddy said drunkenly, whipping the spit off his chin where he'd slobbered. They went out and down the street singing off-key. Noisily entering the hotel lobby, they made straight for the bar.

Lou, probably the youngest of the four, turned to his companions and said, "Boys, let's show these city bastards how us mountain ridge-runners can really drink. Make it four boilermakers," he demanded of Frank, the bartender. Setting their drinks in front of them, Frank shook his head in reproach. They looked pretty drunk already.

Lifting his glass, Lou said, "Down the hatch, boys, and if you think you're man enough to down another, I'll buy." They drained their glasses. Boys, let's drink to the 'cat-walk.'"

Raising his glass in his hand, he edged across the kitchen floor, balancing himself in an exaggerated mimicry of the 'catwalk.' His companions howled. Willard's wife heard them from her bedroom, but just ground her teeth in anger and left them alone.

She awakened them at six o'clock the next morning, or rather three of them. They lay sprawled across the kitchen table, except for Willard. He had managed to make it to the daybed in the living room.

"Come on, you sun lizards, it's time to go to work," she yelled at them. Shaking Lou vigorously by the shoulder, she finally got him awake. He managed to get the other two on their feet, and they headed for the diner. She just let Willard sleep. She could hear him snoring loudly, and she'd be damned if she was going to take another beating trying to rouse him out of his drunken stupor. She didn't even bother to make her own breakfast.

She knew how mean Willard would be when he woke up with a hangover. Instead, she went out, started up their old car, and headed down the road toward her mother's.

Lou and his two friends entered the diner and made haste for the men's room. Lou splattered puke all over the toilet while the other two splashed their faces and heads with cold water. Feeling somewhat better a few minutes later, they lined up at the counter. Wiping the sweat off his forehead, Lou gave his order.

"Make mine tomato juice, Lea, and damn it, make it cold." The other two ordered coffee, black. Three-quarters of an hour later, they were on their job.

"Where's Willard?" their foreman demanded.

"Now, for cripes' sake, would we know?" Lou asked. "Probably home to bed with his pretty wife. You wouldn't be in a hurry to get up either if you had something like that to sleep with, would you?" he prodded.

The foreman eyed them a little suspiciously. They didn't look drunk, but they sure as hell looked like they'd made a night of it somehow. "Oh, well," he silently added, "they had worked on the core-wall ever since it was started, and he sure couldn't afford to give them their time and put somebody new on the job now.

They ought to just about finish it today." The engineer had estimated the wall framework would be done in four months, but with all the delays they'd had in getting material, it had been five already. He'd just have to let the boys work, he decided.

"Alright!" he ordered. "You guys get up there and get started, and no fooling around either. Just remember this," he continued, "it's sixty feet to the ground and the same to Heaven."

Slipping his toolkit over his arm and shoulder, Lou led the way up to the 'cat-walk.' Working diligently, they welded and bolted the cables as necessary. Twice, the foreman managed to get away from his other work to come up and inspect the work on the 'catwalk.'

"By cripes," he said to himself, "they might have had a night of it, but it sure as hell doesn't interfere with their work."

It was nearing noon. The sun seemed to beat down on the men in waves. The damn steel helmets didn't help any, either. They swore it was so hot you could fry an egg on them. Lou passed his hand over his eyes, wiping the sweat out of them. He swore he'd never drink another boilermaker as long as he lived. He was really hungover. Drinking that damn tomato juice in the diner this morning hadn't done anything to help the queasiness in his guts, either. He tightened another bolt on a cable.

Suddenly, a wave of nausea riddled his belly. The cable he was holding onto grew slippery in his damn grip. Dizzily, he tried to wipe the blackness out of his eyes. His buddy glanced up from where he was welding a couple of feet away.

"Lou, hang on!" he yelled, making a futile reach for him just an inch too short and a second too late. Lou's body plummeted downward without a sound until it hit the ground with a dull thud. Taking in the situation at a glance, the foreman shouted to the men on the catwalk, "Come on down, the rest of you. Easy, one at a time."

Pale and shaking, they made it to the ground, joining the workers near Lou's body. The emergency first aid crew arrived in a matter of minutes. But anyone, just anyone, could glance at that crumpled heap and see there was no life in it. The emergency crew filed a D.O.A. report. The core wall had taken its toll.

Lou's two buddies were knocked off work. To hell with schedules, to hell with everything. They headed for Jhan's. They couldn't absorb the fact that Lou was dead. He had been as agile as a slinky panther. He had never missed a step before. The three of them had hunted and fished together since they had been knee-high to a grasshopper. Lou had been the surest-footed, most daring of them all. Disbelief was written all over their pale faces.

The wail of an ambulance siren sounded in the thin air. It sent a cold shiver over the two 'catwalkers' as they sat at the bar. The ambulance careened down Main Street. "Carrying Lou's body away," was their unvoiced opinion, but as it turned out, an incorrect one.

An hour later, the town was rife with the news of a second death in a matter of hours. The ambulance had been wailing its way to pick up the living, not the dead. That's what the emergency crew had assumed, at least. With one look at the purplish face of the sprawled body on the daybed, they doubted.

Willard lay quiet in the same position as when his wife had left him that morning, but there was no noisy snoring. There was no noise at all when she returned at noon. The deadly quiet of the house didn't seem in keeping with Willard's usual hangovers. Leaving the kitchen door wide open to get rid of the stale liquor stench, she went into the living room.

The ugly purplish mottle on her husband's face sent her screaming back out the door like a demented creature.

Some diligent soul called old Doc, and someone else called the emergency squad. They arrived simultaneously. Doc examined the body and decided they'd have to notify the coroner in the next town. He explained that while it seemed Willard had been in good health, he had still apparently succumbed to a heart attack.

"I can't be sure, though," Doc admitted honestly. "I can't sign a death certificate legally until there's an autopsy done."

Willard's widow emitted a weird, moaning cry. "I won't let you do it, Doc," she screamed. "I always threatened to cut his heart out and show it to him, but I didn't mean it. I didn't, I didn't. Please don't cut him up, Doc. I can't stand it." She sobbed hysterically.

Doc motioned for one of the emergency crew to take hold of her. "Beats hell how a woman can take on so over a man that treated her like he did." Doc kept his thoughts to himself as he prepared a hypodermic needle. "Hold your arm still, Mary. This will make you feel better and hurts no more than a bee sting."

Doc plunged the needle swiftly into the soft flesh of her arm. Glancing over the neighbor women gathered around, he commanded, "Now, one of you ladies take her home and stay with her for the time being. She'll go to sleep for a while, and that's what she needs most right now."

Two of the women put their arms around Mary protectively and led her away.

The next day, the coroner's report was spread high, wide, and handsomely all over town. No one seemed to know how the findings leaked out so fast or who started telling about it in the first place. The tale lost nothing in the telling. The sum and substance of the rumors, however, told, remained the same.

The coroner reportedly found Willard's heart split wide open. The heavy drinking the night before was the cause. Death was the effect. The relativity was plain.

Two days later, the work was completed on the 'cat-walk.' There was no celebration as previously planned. Neither were Lou's two buddies around. No one knew where they had gone, but a trucker said he'd met them on the other side of the mountain a couple of weeks later. They had signed on with the tunnel rats. No more sky-scraping for them, they'd vowed vehemently.

The Door Flew Open—So Did the Truth

"Hey, Grace, I..." said Pinky.

Her voice suddenly trailed off when she opened swiftly the swing door to the butler's pantry, catching the long-nosed head waiter smack in the face.

"My God, Mr. Jerome, I'm sorry. I was looking for Grace. I didn't see you here." Pinky set her tray of glasses on the table with shaking hands.

"How many times have I told you to stop pushing that door open with your—ah—posterior, Pinky? In the three months you've been here, you haven't registered a thing I've tried to teach you. I simply can't imagine what Mrs. Losinger was thinking when she hired you in the first place.

If it weren't for Grace Hill covering up your countless mistakes, you would have been fired after the first week. A pretty face and no brains, phaugh! One would think, by watching you wait tables, that you were working in a beanery instead of the best resort in the Catskills."

Running out of breath, Jerome grabbed a piece of ice from the tray on the table and held it to his rapidly swelling nose.

"Like I said, I'm sorry, Mr. Jerome. I thought Grace was in here, and I wanted to ask her if I should put ice in these glasses." Pinky was practically in tears.

"Sorry, sorry," Jerome mimicked her. That's all I hear from you—you—" he stuttered, trying to think of an appropriate invective and failing. You cattle," he finally added contemptuously, "all of you, and

I mean all of you!" He amplified, catching a glimpse of the waitresses and busboys gathered just outside the kitchen door. Scullery maids have better manners than you," he finished insultingly.

His words and gestures took in the entire group. None of them offered to venture inside the kitchen to either aid or pacify him. He was disliked wholeheartedly by all of the waitresses and busboys, not because he was their immediate supervisor, but for his arrogant manner when he gave them orders.

He never let them forget that he had in many fine manor houses in England before emigrating to this country and had been in charge of all the servants, down to the lowly scullery maids. That, in his opinion, made him more than a mere servant.

Seeing the group's unsympathetic and hostile faces staring at him caused Jerome to lose the last vestige of his cool dignity to his hot English temper. He waved his waiter's towel frenziedly about, then held it to his face as blood started dribbling from his nose, spotting his stiffly starched shirt front.

"He's going to get his nose smashed again for saying that," Eddie Bischer, one of the busboys, said angrily and started to push his way past Grace Hill into the kitchen.

"Stay out of there," she whispered, laying a restraining hand on his arm. "He'll wham the hell out of you and you'll lose your job besides."

Perturbed by the momentary lull in the main dining room service, Mrs. Losinger rose from her table and made her way inconspicuously across the room and down the hall to the kitchen. Her peremptory, "What's going on here?" scattered the group, including a suddenly nonbelligerent Eddie, away from the kitchen door, giving her a full view of the head waiter's hysterics and the cowering Pinky.

Hastily taking in the scene, she picked up the extension phone and ordered the service desk to send in the second head waiter and the house doctor.

"I don't think it's fractured, Jerome," she said soothingly as she ran her finger gingerly along the once aquiline bridge of his nose. "I don't know, though, it's terribly swollen," she added dubiously, gently maneuvering him down on a stool and reapplying the towel with ice.

Jerome tried to sniff haughtily but only achieved a nauseous gagging sound from the blood dribbling down the back of his throat.

Pinky's small voice broke through the sound of Jerome's gagging. "I'm sorry, truly sorry, Mrs. Losinger, but how could I possibly know he was standing behind the door? I backed through because my hands were full. I was in a hurry and—well, that's how it happened," she stammered tearfully.

Before Mrs. Losinger could reply, Jerome made a strangling noise in his throat and started to gesticulate wildly. "I'll not work another day with her," he finally gurgled. Mrs. Losinger laid a placating hand on his shoulder, then moved aside as the doctor entered the kitchen.

"Oh. There you are. Thank heaven," she said relievedly.

The doctor ran quick exploratory fingers over Jerome's nose and face. "There's no need for an x-ray, Mrs. Losinger. It's definitely not fractured, just badly bruised. It should be as good as new in a few days. Keep ice compresses on it and take one of these tablets every three or four hours for pain if you need to."

He handed Jerome a packet of pills and turned to Mrs. Losinger. "Perhaps he should stay out of the dining room for a week or so, Mrs. Losinger. He's going to have a couple of shiners out of this too. Otherwise, there is nothing serious."

"Thank you, Doctor. Of course, you will look in on him daily until he can return to his duties."

"Certainly, Mrs. Losinger, if it will reassure you," the doctor consented in a rather obsequious manner, which wasn't foreign to him in Mrs. Losinger's presence.

Too much of his professional dignity and top medical skills had slipped insidiously, but nonetheless definitely, in his gradually increased consumption of cocktails in his former role of a New York society doctor. Consequently, his practice hadn't merely suffered from his remissness of duty but finally ceased to exist. Necessity had eventually forced him to accept his present position at Losinger's hotel.

It seemed to him that of late, Mrs. Losinger's attitude toward him had taken on that quality shown by a mistress to her menial servants. His heart and soul shriveled in humiliation, but his willpower to straighten himself out had long ago succumbed to, and shrouded itself thereafter, in a haze of alcohol.

"Damn Jerome and everybody else," he muttered to himself after leaving the kitchen and gaining the empty corridor. Mrs. Losinger seemed unusually thoughtful for a few minutes after his departure, then regained her usual stern composure. She ordered rather than asked Jerome to retire to his room.

"I'll stop by in a little while to see if you need anything," she informed him in tones that brooked no arguments.

Completely mollified, Jerome rose from his stool. "Thank you, Mrs. Losinger," he mumbled through swollen lips.

Mentally tabulating the worth of her temperamental head waiter and the trembling Pinky, Mrs. Losinger turned to her and commanded sternly, "Pinky, go to my office and wait for me. I'll be along in a few minutes."

"Yes, ma'am," Pinky answered meekly. Glad to escape, she rushed blindly out of the kitchen, unmindful of Jerome's oft-repeated admonitions, and collided with a figure in the doorway. Momentarily knocked out of breath from the impact, she was squarely enveloped in a pair of arms until she regained her balance. A bit longer and closer than necessary, Pinky thought as Ben Losinger grinned down at her. His grin faded to a sickly grimace when he looked up and caught the suspicious stare of his wife.

"There now," he said, pushing Pinky hurriedly away, "see that you're a bit more careful in the future."

Pinky, subdued and quiet, went on to the office. "That! If nothing else, did it," she thought ruefully. There goes my job and any chance I had of meeting that talent scout Eddie was telling me about. Damn that miserable old Losinger anyway." With a clenched fist, she wiped the tears from her stormy eyes.

The sound of the office door opening softly brought her around to face Mrs. Losinger as she entered the room regally.

"Of course, Pinky, you realize you are dismissed," she said without preamble. "Nor, in view of your past and present behavior," she continued loftily, "can I give you a recommendation elsewhere." Seating herself at her desk, she filled in a check and handed it to Pinky. "You are being reimbursed in lieu of the usual two weeks' notice, and," she continued emphatically, "you are to leave this hotel immediately. I'll call a taxi for you when you're ready, say at two o'clock." She glanced at her wristwatch.

"That gives you a bit over an hour to pack." "Oh, there is one more thing," her voice halted Pinky as she started out the door. Pinky turned inquiringly. "Yes?" she asked, with a hint of both tears and anger in her voice.

"I can do without the impertinence, Pinky. I merely wanted to advise you not to seek work in any of the nearby hotels. Our type of hotel needs more than a pretty face and sexy figure to wait tables, which seems contrary to your ideas."

She glanced up and down at Pinky's lush figure contemptuously, then continued her tirade. "You lack poise and the intelligence, it appears, to develop it. Your mind is everywhere but on your work. You are absolutely and completely incompetent."

Her sharp rebuke finally whip-lashed Pinky into an angry retort.

"I told you I was inexperienced when you hired me, Mrs. Losinger, and while you may consider it a handicap, your husband certainly doesn't seem to, though I wouldn't spit on him," she finished indignantly, slamming the door on Mrs. Losinger's reply.

Grace Hill was waiting for Pinky when she reached her room. "Pink, what happened?" she asked concernedly.

Pinky untied her frill of an apron and threw it on the bed before answering. "Don't tell me you can't guess," she said sarcastically.

"I'm fired, Grace. In no uncertain terms, I'm fired! Not only for banging that icicle of a Jerome in the nose or for being incompetent as that witch would like me to believe, but mainly because I landed accidentally in old Ben Losinger's paws on my way out of the kitchen. Well, I didn't see him in the damn doorway," she said defensively as Grace lifted her eyebrow inquiringly.

"I bumped into him and he clung like a cocklebur. Of course, Mrs. Losinger witnessed it all. You could almost hear the old wolf lick his chops. I was finished working here right then, and I knew it."

"Well, I'm sorry, Pinky," Grace sympathized. "That old goat has made a pass at all of the waitresses at one time or another. It's too bad that Mrs. Losinger happened to be on the spot this time, though. Then again, maybe it's better she was, at least for your sake."

"I can't see how it benefited me," Pinky exclaimed. "The most I got out of the deal was getting fired."

"As I said, maybe you were lucky, even if you can't see it." Grace looked indecisive for a moment, then apparently making up her mind, continued.

"I've never told this to anyone, Pinky, but I'm going to tell you for your own benefit. Ben Losinger can be hard to handle. He won't stop at anything short of knocking a girl out to get what he wants, and you know what that is. I know because it was when I first came here that I had a tussle with him. In fact, I almost drowned him."

"What in, a highball?" Pinky asked derisively. "You don't expect me to believe that one, now do you, Grace? You sound just like my mother when she tells one of her old wives' tales."

"You'd be better off if you would listen to your mother once in a while, young lady. Because you've reached the ripe old age of eighteen, you think you know all the answers, but you've a long way to go yet."

"I'm sorry, Grace. I didn't mean to be fresh. Tell me what happened." Grace looked at her for a moment, half angry for the moment.

"As I told you, it occurred last summer." Grace paused reflectively, then continued. "He followed me out to the pool one night, or I think he did. At any rate, he arrived right after I did. It was around midnight and so hot I couldn't get to sleep, so I decided to take a dip in the pool to cool off. I didn't think anyone would be around at that time, but I had no sooner gotten in the water when he loomed up at the pool entrance.

"He really looked funny standing there in the moonlight, with his broomstick legs and knobby knees sticking out of those scanty shorts he affects. I was too darn scared to laugh, though. I stayed on the opposite side of the pool as long as I could, but I got so cold I finally had to get out," she said.

There was a pause.

"I had to pass him, and when I did, he grabbed me. I struggled to get loose, but he kept bending me over backward and kissing me. I couldn't scream, he kept his slobbering old mouth tight against mine. He also managed to get his hand down inside my swimsuit." Grace shivered in revulsion, then continued.

"All of a sudden, I got over being scared and was fighting mad. I pretended I liked his pawing, went sort of limp, and pushed up against him real close. That edged him closer to the pool, and I tripped him, giving him a hard shove at the same time. He landed ass over tin cup in the water.

Another pause.

"He let loose of me just in time, or I'd have landed right on top of him. I didn't know if he could swim or not, and right then, I didn't give a damn. To top it all off, I heard someone coming," she said.

"I was scared half out of my wits and ducked into that clump of shrubbery by the gate. I could hear old Losinger floundering and sputtering to beat hell in the water and saw the night watchman as he came along and helped him out. He told the watchman he'd been taking a walk around the pool and must have slipped on a piece of broken cement along the edge," she said.

"The watchman waited until he got out of hearing, then cussed him out, saying something about a lying old bastard," she complained, paused and continued.

"I'm positive he must have seen most of it, but he's never mentioned it to me. Old Losinger has never said anything either, and he knows I wouldn't dare, not if I want to keep on working here. He lies to Mrs. Losinger right to her teeth, and she believes everything he says. I notice lately that every time I wait on their table, he makes some snide remark about the service. He's very subtle about it, but all the same, Mrs. Losinger keeps watching me rather speculatively. He wants to have her fire me, and that's how he's going about it, without coming right out and saying so."

"It's just as well to get fired as you have been because you would have been later, anyway. That is, unless you let him have his way with you," Grace said bluntly. "And even with that," she added, "Mrs. Losinger has a way of rectifying things eventually. You'll be in real trouble." She rose, butted her cigarette, and opened the door.

"Wait a minute, Grace, I've got an idea," Pinky said impulsively. "Why don't you quit? You say you don't like it here anyway, and we'll look for another job together? They're building another reservoir down around Pine Bush somewhere to connect somehow with the one in Gainesville, and I hear the hotels and restaurants down there are practically begging for help. I don't think they pay as well as here, but the tips are better."

"Sorry, kid," Grace refused, "but I have other plans. Go home and grow up some more," she ended not unkindly. "Gosh, if I don't get back to work, I'll get canned along with you. Take it easy and lots of luck," Grace called back as she hurried down the hall. Pinky started packing her old cardboard suitcase.

"I covered for you in the dining room, Grace," one of the other waitresses called out as Grace came into the kitchen. "Mrs. Losinger didn't bother to come back, so you weren't even missed."

"Thanks, Zelda. I'll finish up," Grace replied. Balancing a tray of desserts high on her hand, she left the kitchen.

The rest of the lunch period seemed to drag on interminably to Grace, but finally, the last guest left the dining room, and the waitresses took their afternoon break.

Grace made a telephone call and then went to her room. With tears very near the surface, she flung herself across the bed.

"The damn men are all alike," she thought as Gene's image was projected in her mind's eye. "Now I know why he hasn't called me or been over." She tried not to think of the phone conversation she had just had with him, but it was impossible. It had taken a few minutes before he finally answered the insistent ringing. He had sounded half-drunk and half-mad when he heard her voice.

"We're busy, really pushing on the job, and I have to get some rest," Gene had explained in answer to her anxious questioning as to why he hadn't gotten in touch with her. At the same time, he said, "You do understand, don't you, baby?" Grace heard a girl's throaty laugh in the background.

"He's got another woman in the trailer with him." Grace quietly hung up the receiver. "I'd recognize that laugh of Polly Howe's anywhere. Somehow I knew it would be like this." Her thoughts scattered through her mind, remembering his excuses for not getting a divorce.

The dozens of times when he hadn't shown up when they had a date. "Well, that's that and enough of this mooning," Grace muttered aloud, getting up from the bed.

"Talking to yourself? That's the beginning of nowhere, my pet. Ready for the evening grind?" Zelda Wells stood in the doorway of Grace's room, laughing.

"Oh, I didn't hear you knock," Grace said, startled.

"Of course you didn't because I didn't," Zelda retorted. "Better step on it, kiddo. We're due in the slave quarters in exactly ten minutes."

"Wait a minute and I'll walk down with you," Grace said, smearing a dab of lipstick across her mouth.

"You're sure looking perky. What did you do, take a nap?" Grace asked Zelda half-jestingly on their way to the kitchen.

"Whoever heard of such nonsense?" Zelda scoffed. "Of course I didn't. I shampooed and set my hair, and while I had the dryer on it, I did my nails. Don't tell me you can't see the difference after spending all that time on this mop of mine." She patted her auburn curls caressingly.

"Your hair always looks beautiful, and you know it," Grace complimented her. "By the way, is Jed coming over tonight?"

"Of course," Zelda replied. "You've never seen him pass up a chance to date me yet, have you?"

"You sound real confident, Zelda, but—" Zelda interrupted her hastily.

"Heavens, Grace, we've only three minutes to make the kitchen. Come on, for goodness' sake. We'll gab later."

"Grace, I've got an idea," Zelda said as she tonged ice expertly into a tray of glasses a few minutes later in the pantry. "Jed won't be here before nine tonight. He's going to meet me at Tony's Bar. Oh, you know the place I mean," she explained to Grace's puzzled look. "It's directly across the highway from the lower gate."

"Oh, that place. Yeah, go on," Grace replied.

"Why not doll up and walk over with me as soon as we've finished serving dinner? We'll have a chance to talk for an hour before Jed gets here. A little ol' highball might pick you up a bit, too. Besides, you've looked a bit seedy these last couple of weeks, and a little relaxation is in order. Say yes, will you," Zelda urged, "or is Gene coming over?" She quirked an arched eyebrow at Grace.

"No, Gene isn't coming over, and yes, it's a date," Grace assented as she lifted the water pitcher and filled the crystal glasses.

"Someday I'll be setting my own table with thirty-five-dollar glasses just like these," Zelda remarked flippantly, flicking her fingernails against one to hear it ring. "I just bet you will," Grace replied. "That glitter in your eyes isn't a reflection of these glasses."

"Why try to be a lamb if you're on the market, honey. Don't you know by now that lambs eventually wind up in the slaughterhouse?" Zelda laughed scornfully as she pushed open the heavy door to the dining room.

The two girls faded into mere serviceable shadows in the luxuriously carpeted, softly lighted room. The second-head waiter, filled with importance at his chance of substituting for Jerome, kept a keen and ever-watchful eye on the waitresses and busboys. The low cadence of the diners' voices seemed tuned to the soft strains of the Viennese waltz played by the string orchestra partly hidden by huge potted palms.

"They look like suited penguins in slow motion," Grace had once said of the orchestra when describing the atmosphere of the dining room to Gene.

Now, the same fanciful allusion crossed her mind again as the soft tempo of the music caught and pulled at her emotions. Encountering a direct look from Ben Losinger as she passed his table dispelled everything from her mind except the immediate task of serving the guests deftly and withdrawing to the pantry between courses.

"Thank the Lord for small favors," she said fervently as she and Zelda were preparing to serve the desserts. The other waitresses hadn't arrived back in the pantry yet, and for the moment, the two were alone.

"Amen," Zelda kidded irreverently, "but what's the favor?"

"I'm just thankful that I didn't get the Losingers at one of my tables tonight. I'd have wound up pouring the soup down his neck. I can't stand the sight of him tonight."

"You're simply upset because you think it was his fault that Pinky got fired this noon. It wasn't altogether that, you know. Everyone knew you watched over her like an old mother hen, covering up for her and doing half her work. It's a miracle she wasn't fired out of here weeks ago," she said.

"She was just a movie-struck kid. She couldn't keep an order straight in that pretty head of hers, no matter what. Besides, she simply wasn't cut out for this kind of work. Eddie Bischer might have nicknamed her Bumpy for quite another reason, but it fitted her well all the same. I never, in my life, seen anyone so awkward. She never saw anything until she bumped into it."

"Well!" Grace exclaimed. "Are you finished? Now, let me tell you something. My aversion for Ben Losinger doesn't stem from anything relating to Pinky. He's a completely ruthless, immoral, sickening old man." Grace, flushed and angry, suddenly ceased her berating of Ben. Catching the dawning, knowing look in Zelda's eyes, she realized she may have said too much already.

"So—that's the way it is," Zelda speculated.

"Oh, it's nothing personal," Grace answered. "I think I must have been born despising his type," she finished lamely.

"Forget it," Zelda advised. "Now, if you really want to see something, just take a gander at the way our little 'busboy Eddie' is fawning over that Broadway talent scout when you go back to the dining room. I forgot to tell you in all the excitement this noon that this particular scout arranged a sort of audition for Eddie this evening right after dinner. Mrs. Losinger informed one of the other boys to take over Eddie's duties. She said Eddie was going to sing with the orchestra."

"Maybe this is Eddie's chance to make the big time, Zelda. He does sing like a nightingale."

"Yeah," Zelda admitted, "but if he gets anywhere with this particular scout, he's going to make like a fairy as well. That guy is a queer if I've ever seen one. He'll get Eddie started in a career alright, but first, he'll insist that Eddie go through an orientation period that includes sharing a cozy, little apartment in New York with him. You were concerned about Pinky meeting him, and all the time the miserable little freak wouldn't touch a female with a ten-foot pole."

Grace shrugged and replied, "If you ask me, Zelda, Eddie is a bright boy and a poor one. If that is how he proposes to get on top of the ladder, forget about it. He won't be the first nor the last to do it. Let's not wait for his grand finale tonight. I'd rather get something to eat over at Tony's than wait around here for an hour after he's done singing, just to eat a dinner that I don't want anyway."

"OK by me," Zelda nodded as she left the pantry.

"Never did I see people take so long to eat," Grace said grumpily to Zelda as they finished serving and left the dining room.

"Why not?" Zelda replied cynically. "They're paying for atmosphere. They may as well enjoy it. Now I've had enough of this place for one day, Grace. Let's forget it exists. We've not much time to dilly-dally if we expect to get to Tony's ahead of Jed."

"I'll be showered and dressed before you will. In fact, I'll bet you a drink on it," Grace challenged.

"You're on," Zelda laughed as she banged her room door shut.

THE BOOM FADES, THE BURN REMAINS

THE INHABITANTS OF Gainesville were now like shifting desert sands.

People came and went, nothing and no one stayed permanently. Property was bought and sold, razed or improved as whim dictated. It was an oasis for salesmen thirsting for business, and money changed hands quickly, spent indiscriminately by most.

The common laborer made as much money in a week as he once made in a month. It was commonplace to see the latest model cars moving in and out of town, driven by people dressed in either dirty sweatshirts and dungarees or well-pressed suits.

Business had mushroomed, and just about anything could be bought or sold, legally or illegally. The town had a soiled look, like newly fallen snow dirtied here and there by a careless person. A few old-timers deplored its present state, but most inhabitants couldn't care less.

Morals grew lax as money became plentiful. Though the connection was nebulous, it was there. There had been an influx of people, new ideas, and a completely new standard of living introduced to the town. Most of the original inhabitants conformed and adjusted to the new pattern, while only a paltry few clung to their old way of existence, and the minority didn't count.

The town was on a spree. People worked, danced, and drank until the wee hours of the morning. If their laughter carried a note of hysteria, it was just an accompaniment to the birth of a boom town. Evolution came at a fairly fast, steady pace. The Shaw Building, housing the drug store and bank on its first floor, was razed.

Venerable Mr. Wilson retired with his memories. An old building that had years ago served as a clothing store, with living quarters upstairs, situated half a block down from the bank, was sold to an out-of-town druggist. Marjorie Holmes, its owner, was glad to rid herself of the responsibility of ownership. At the age of thirty, with a pimpled face and overweight, she had been placed in the town's category of 'old maid,' though definitely part of its social upper strata.

That is, she was part of it until she started tipping the bottle after her crusty bachelor brother died three years ago, and she inherited the building.

She gradually emerged from her secret imbibing at home to become part of Jhan's Cafe society. Red-faced and bleary-eyed, she'd sit there night after night, extending her pinky away from her highball glass in a curved dainty gesture befitting one of the Holmes. When she sold the store, she rented a two-room apartment, not too large but large enough to assuage her compulsions.

Maggie eventually found herself faced with a competitor. Renovated, with a modern imposing front bearing foot-high gold and black lettering reading "Pharmacy" across its plate glass window, Marjorie's old building was now listed on the tax roll as the property of Wallace Wynkool, a young but enterprising pharmacist fresh out of college. Sharing part of the pharmacy's first floor were the offices of Dr. Styles.

The town had finally drawn the interest of a young doctor who liked small towns and the lack of future competition he'd face in a town with its only doctor on the shady side of seventy. He was gradually accepted by the townspeople, not only for his charming bedside manner but for his skill and ability as a medical man. Old Doc retired to a more or less sedentary existence.

Main Street began to take on the appearance of a soiled oil painting that had been partially cleaned in a haphazard fashion, then cast aside as a bad job. An occasional new or renovated building here and there, sandwiched between some of the older ones, had handsome facades that only served to detract from the street's attractiveness.

The bank, ousted from its former quarters, decided out of pride and its capital gain of five years to have a new building constructed specifically for banking purposes and nothing else. On a hitherto barren plot of ground next to the new pharmacy, a red brick building was erected. Small evergreens primly decorated the walk leading to the grilled door that centered the brick-and-mortar facade of the bank building.

The bank established a new innovation to its banking system by instituting a cashier's cage on the left side of its main floor with a window opening to the black-topped drive that passed it, arcing in a half circle that led back to the street again. Patrons could do much of their business via the cashier's window without leaving their car.

On the first day of the bank's official opening to the public, Martin Dulle, its president, unlocked the door with a dignity swelled by surety and confidence that he hadn't manifested in either himself or the bank six years before.

He noticed that his two female cashiers also seemed to have an air about them as they stood behind their cage windows. He decided they looked trim and efficient, but his nerves shattered whenever they had occasion to walk across the room. The staccato click of their new high heels on the tile floor disrupted the quietness he felt was mandatory in a bank. Besides, it always focused his attention on their legs.

It was ironic that he should think of Maggie because of this, completely out of keeping with his position, but he did. Spurred by the actions taken by the pharmacist and bank director, the manager of the now non-existent movie house incited enough interest in his business associates to finance the building of a new one.

Apparently, the financial backers of the movie venture weren't interested in beautifying the town or creating dramatic effects with a pretentious or expensive building. They hired a contractor to slap together a large Quonset-type aluminum building bought second-hand from Army surplus.

Completed, it resembled a discarded and forgotten barracks as it sat on a partly cleared lot at the junction of Main Street and the newly constructed road that led to the east end of the dam sector. The manager, however, contracted for more recent and popular movie productions to entice the public. By displaying picture previews that covered most of the theater's front, he contrived to compensate for the lack of elegance in its appearance. Considering the price of admission had increased to double the former fee, the patronage was excellent.

The town seemed to be awakening out of its tipsy lethargic state. So far, it was but a yawning and stretching wakefulness, but the school board, for one, began to see the handwriting on the wall. They decided to get in first with the most before the town woke up completely and started a general overhauling. Their own seats on the school board would be in jeopardy then.

Desiring to hold onto their presently esteemed and coveted status, they called a meeting to see what could be accomplished toward building a new school. The present building had long been inadequate for the ever-swelling enrollment. They presented the resulting minutes of the meeting to the town and met with unanimous agreement.

The state education department, upon being presented with the town's formal application for financial aid for the new school, finally acquiesced to its demands. Within two years, an architect's dream was realized in a contemporary building of yellow brick and cement situated at the extreme end of Maple Street on the east side of town.

Whereas the old high school had once frowned down on Gainesville in arrogant hauteur, this new one seemed to beckon one nearer, to invite one to cross its landscaped grounds and enter its friendly portals to absorb the wealth of knowledge to be found within. Perchance, the sun that hung like a suspended golden ball over its dome for part of the day gave the impression of gracious warmth that greeted the passer-by.

The school board felt this was the psychological moment to sit back and rest on its laurels. They were certain to be reappointed next term for their meritorious endeavor in progressive education. They were jarred out of their complacency, however, to learn at their next meeting that the professorial duties in the school would not be carried out by Prof. Tague.

He submitted his resignation at that time, effective at the close of the present school semester. He stated matter-of-factly that he had been appointed to the state's regents board in the capital and that he considered himself lucky. It was with pained regret that the school board accepted his resignation.

It was with exultance that the B.W.S. bought the old school building and prepared to establish permanent auxiliary offices there in the interest of the dam's future. A bit of refurbishing would be ideal for their purposes.

Work on the dam project went steadily forward. Shafts were sunk, and the tunnel rats blasted the main tunnel's route through mountains that were virtually rock beds a few feet beneath the surface. Shaft number one tunnel, with its starting point just above Gainesville, and shaft number four tunnel, commencing thirty miles beyond it and north of the Manor, were constantly progressing toward each other. The day arrived when the tunnel rats in both tunnels could hear the resounding noise of the others' tools as they worked.

Driving up in his ancient red Ford with a conspicuous number thirteen painted on its door for luck, honest Jed was on hand to observe the breakthrough of the two tunnels. Descending the mid-way shaft, he stood poised expectantly beside Carmen and two other junior engineers. The last few feet of dirt fell away between the two tunnels, and the tunnel rats emerged from a common opening.

Pandemonium broke loose as Jed handed every fifth one a bottle of liquor and ordered them above. As the last man ascended, Jed turned to Carmen and the two other engineers, holding out his hand. "You bastards will learn," honest Jed laughed as they each laid fifty dollars in his hand.

"I could have bet my life you were off five feet back there in number one tunnel, Jed," remarked Carmen. The other two looked at Jed, respectively.

"You're an old dog, Jed," one of the men laughed.

"Don't complain, boys," Jed said smugly. "It only costs you fifty bucks to learn a very simple feat of engineering."

While the plans for the tunnel had been beyond the layman's comprehension, also casting some doubt among his associates, honest Jed knew exactly what he was doing. He'd bet his life on his expected results. Looking down at the tunnel's opening, the other three engineers felt the same way. There wasn't a fraction of an inch variance in the joining of the two tunnels that now formed a thirty-mile straight unit.

Eventually, it would be part of the Gainesville dam system, carrying water through to an auxiliary dam at Lackawack.

Honest Jed and his companions ascended the shaft, had a round of drinks with the tunnel rats, and gave them the rest of the afternoon off with pay to celebrate the tunnel's completion. By nightfall, every tunnel rat was roaring drunk. Their tunnel foreman had thrown them a party, complete with dinner and all the liquor they could drink.

Old Maggie entertained three of them that night. After the last one left, she admitted to herself that she had been too poor lately to take on one after another like that. "That last one had been a bull, though," she comforted herself. She could still hear him cussing her roundly and savagely, swearing he wouldn't pay her. She had finally managed to satisfy him, and he threw two dollars on the table and left.

Maggie locked the door behind him, picked up the two dollars, and shoved it down in the top of her stocking along with the five she'd managed to filch from his pants pocket where he had flung them on the floor. Catching a glimpse of her reflection in the mirror over the kitchen sink, she paused to stare for a moment.

Voicing a string of vile epithets, she ran her hand over her face, bringing it away to peer closely at the palm. There was nothing on it except sweat. Talking to herself, she swore aloud that some of the bastards that frequented her place were half-Jap, and their color was wearing off on her. She had noticed for weeks now how yellow her skin was getting. Even the whites of her eyes had turned yellow.

"Damn 'em," she muttered, pouring a glass of liquor and drinking it. Bubbles of gas started rolling around in her belly almost as soon as she swallowed the liquor. Remembering a story one of the girls had told her about stocks, she leaned over the back of a chair and laughed to herself. "Let yer American gas go," she chortled as a sharp crack sounded in the room. "There, that helped some."

Grimacing, she straightened up, only to be violently sick to her stomach the next minute. She heaved up the liquor and continued retching for another ten minutes.

"Guess I'll have to go see that new doctor," she thought ruefully as she flung herself on the cot, completely spent. One of the girls that hung out at Maggie's found her the next morning. Bloated and ugly, she lay there with big splotches of dried blood all over the pillow, her face, and the hand she had apparently used to wipe away the blood from her smeared mouth.

"I don't know what else she was, but she sure was a drinker," the coroner stated after the autopsy. "Death was due to rupture of the liver," he explained to his aide.

Jake watched from the restaurant window as the funeral cortege went down the street. "Just two cars and the hearse," he counted to himself. The restaurant was deserted except for Jake and Jess. Not bothering to get up from his stool at the counter, Jess stretched his neck to catch a glimpse of the cars as they passed by.

"Don't fret, Jake," he advised, "there's plenty of it left around here. Besides, we're damn lucky we weren't up there the night it happened." The hearse continued through the town with its pauper burial of old Maggie.

Jake moved away from the window to the back of the counter. Disregarding Jess's allusion to Maggie, he broke the unusual silence. "Jess, I've got a chance to sell this restaurant," he said unexpectedly.

"Why, man, you'd be crazy to sell it," Jess answered, looking at him rather startled.

"No, I wouldn't either," Jake denied. "Not at the price I've been offered, at any rate. That new barber down the street wants it. Not for himself. It's his son, really, who wants it, but his old man is staking him. Seems like the boy just passed his bar exams and wants to set up a law practice here in town."

"Well, what the hell would he want with a restaurant then?" Jess demanded.

"It's not the business he wants," Jake enlightened. "It's the building. He likes the location right here in the center of town. Don't you realize," he continued, "that this dam will be finished by this fall?"

"Should be," Jess admitted. "After all, they've been at it six years. But what the hell," he said explosively, "has that got to do with a lawyer wanting to buy this place?"

"Man, you are lost," Jake exclaimed impatiently. "Have you stopped to think that when this dam is completed, this town's business will practically come to a standstill again? Every business will suffer, and eating places will suffer most of all."

"How the hell can three or four of 'em make a living in a town this size when the dam workers leave for good? As for a lawyer settling here, well, that's got good common sense behind it. There'll be people fighting legal claims of one sort or another years from now," he said.

"Yep, if that boy is anywhere near as smart as his father says he is, he should make good money here. I've decided to take the old man's offer and get the hell out of this town. The whole filthy place makes my stomach crawl lately," he finally added.

"You've stomached a lot of things worse than this town, Jake, but who knows, maybe a change will do you good," Jess answered. "I just can't figure you out, Jake. You were always out for strange stuff while you were married to Grace, then after she up and left, you started acting like a love-sick calf. Don't let a little piece of tail get you down. Look at me," Jess laughed, "all the nookie I want when I want it, and I ain't married to no split tail."

"Suppose you're right," Jake mumbled morosely as a customer entered, putting an end to their conversation.

Kisses, Regrets and a Walk That Ends It All

Dr. Shaktel came down the hospital corridor.

He paused by the door of the nurse's station. Becky sat at her desk, finishing notes on the numerous charts. It was nearing the time for the afternoon nursing staff to come on duty and for her to go off duty.

It startled her when Dr. Shaktel put his hand on her shoulder. Absorbed as she was, she had neither seen nor heard his approach. Glancing quickly around, he brushed his lips lightly across her cheek.

"Dinner tonight, Rebecca?" he invited.

For just a second, she felt annoyed; whether with him or herself, she couldn't quite clarify.

"I do need a rest; I'm getting petty," she thought, as a wish filtered through her mind that he would just once call her Becky instead of Rebecca.

"Yes, of course, Louis," she answered him.

"Be ready at six, then. I've some important news to relay to a certain young lady."

The words sort of trailed behind him as he hastened away, but without inspiring either anticipation or curiosity on Becky's part.

She felt remote from the hospital as she walked down the long corridor, going off duty. Still a part of it, though, when she stopped momentarily to sharply reprimand an orderly for handling a tank of oxygen improperly.

"I'm sorry, Miss Hawk," he apologized immediately, tightening a loose strap. She went on down the hall.

Leola, a nurse's aide, bobbed her head around the door of the utility room.

"Psst," Leola looked up. "I heard the super giving you hell," she said. "What happened?"

"I don't know what's ailing her today," Leola complained. "This makes twice I've caught it. She's sure got her talons out. In all the ten years she's been super, I've never seen her like this."

"She's probably got a bug on. Maybe she had a fight with Dr. Shaktel," Leola conjectured. "You know they're sweet on each other."

"About time she married him, then," Leola replied grumpily. "She sure as hell ain't getting any younger or sweeter dispositioned."

"Right about now, you could stand some sugar yourself, Leola," she retorted. "I'll be off duty in ten minutes, and we'll go have a couple of beers. Maybe that'll help. Meet you at the elevator."

Becky felt her irritation dwindling as she started walking the two blocks to her apartment. Even in New York, one caught the freshness of the spring breeze.

Freed now and then from winter's tenacity, it blew in capricious fashion, swooping up a bit of paper, swirling it around and around, pulling on Becky's cape, rustling her stiffly starched uniform. It was like a child escaping the firm hold of its mother's hand, gamboling about, enjoying its momentary freedom. Trying to push aside her nonsensical thoughts and think of more mundane things, Becky entered the apartment building.

"I don't know what's the matter with me today."

Standing inside her living room, her mind automatically registered the click of the lock as she pushed the door shut behind her.

"Anyone knowing me would know my apartment would look exactly like this," she reflected pensively. "Every piece of furniture is correct and in place and clean, almost to the point of being aseptic. I wish just once I could whiff the odor of good old cow shit and the stink of an old barn again." She grinned at the indignity of it, but she glumly admitted silently that it would be preferable to the smells in N.Y.C.

Unfastening her cape, Becky flung it disgustedly on the sofa and slumped down in the chair across from it. She gazed speculatively at the picture of her father and mother. The photograph had been developed from an old tintype taken when they were first married. "Dreams," she said aloud, picking up the picture, then continued in reverie.

"How could I have ever imagined bringing them here? What a child I was. Uprooting their lives would have killed them as surely as the accident."

Her abstracted gaze drifted about the room. "None of this would have made them happier than they already were."

She was pinpointing her thoughts to tangible facts.

"Why, Ma, you and Pa, in your very simplicity, held the core to the purpose of living, to life itself," she added, addressing herself to the picture she was holding. Placing it back on the table, she reflected.

Poverty and hard work didn't stack up harshly for them because it was combined with love and understanding of each other's needs. They were born to the soil, earthy people, living in harmony with God and the land, with themselves.

"I'm glad," she mused, "glad that they died together. Sorry for me, but glad for them. I'm glad I left their spirits to roam free with the winds that blow over the land."

The phone rang. She got up to answer it. It was the hospital. The afternoon supervisor's voice vibrated crisply over the wires.

"It's in the office files, Mrs. Johnson," Becky replied to her question.

"Thank you," the phone clicked.

Becky cradled the receiver impatiently.

"I'm tired of this damn rat race," she stormed silently. "Tired of dating the chief of staff just because he's the chief of staff, and it flatters me. I'm taking an emergency leave of absence. Right this minute."

She repeated it aloud, liking the sound of the words. She looked at Liz and Hiram's picture again as she reached for the phone.

"I know where I'm going, too, Ma!" she cried exultantly.

Less than a half hour after she called the hospital, her doorbell buzzed.

"Rebecca, what happened?" Dr. Shaktel demanded as she held open the door for him.

"Come in, Louis. Sit down. I presume you've heard about my emergency leave. It certainly doesn't take long for the grapevine to start working, does it?" Becky stated rather than asking.

"Well," he started and was interrupted abruptly as Becky hastily continued.

"Louis, it's not the type of emergency you're thinking of, and that's my reason for leaving, but it's an emergency all the same. One that only I, and I alone, can take care of. I'm leaving tonight, and I don't know when or if I'll return, but it has to be."

"You're only serving to confuse me more, Rebecca. Can't you be a bit more specific?" Dr. Shaktel pleaded. "What about our dinner date? Don't you want to hear what I have to tell you?" His eyes held a bleak look as he waited for her answer. Taking advantage of her silence, he continued.

"Surely, Rebecca, you know how much regard I hold you in, how much respect I have for you. Don't tell me you haven't hazarded a guess at the news I wanted to tell you," he said, pulling her down gently beside him on the sofa.

"Truthfully, Louis," Becky replied, "I've been too preoccupied with other things." Please don't ask me, make me humiliate you, she pleaded silently. But Dr. Shaktel persisted.

"Rebecca, this isn't the time or place I had in mind to ask you, but I want you to marry me."

"He'll never lose his dignified, calm, poised manner."

The thought irrelevantly flashed through Becky's mind as she got up, crossed the room, and positioned herself by the closed window. Suddenly, she wanted to smash out the glass and let the breeze billow the curtains, even if it would ruin the correct temperature and coolness of the rooms.

"I'm tired of everything being conditioned, even myself," she thought passionately as she turned to face the man who had just proposed to her and, in doing so, offered her this controlled existence for the rest of her life.

"I'm sorry, Louis," she said bluntly, "but the answer is no. I admire and respect you. I even imagined I might fall in love with you, but I know now that I'm not."

"But, Rebecca," he remonstrated, only to be interrupted by Becky's adamant voice.

"Louis, please, go. Don't make it harder on either of us."

He rose, paused by the door momentarily, "Rebecca, whenever and whatever ails you passes, call me," he said distastefully, closing the door behind him.

"Ever the machine in human guise," Becky reflected, staring at the closed door. "No pleading or lack of self-control even in this moment of rejection. Definitely, he's not earthly enough for me," she thought with finality. "And underneath, I'm much too whimsical for him."

She kicked her slipper off as it flew across the room in sheer exuberance.

SHE LEFT, HE DRANK, THE REST A BLUR

THE B.W.S. OFFICES in the old high school building hummed with activity.

Honest Jed was in high spirits. He laid aside a large map of the dam sector and bundled together a bunch of blueprints. "That's it," he said to his red-headed secretary, patting her familiarly on her fanny as she rose to leave.

Carmen entered Jed's office just in time to catch the scene with Zelda smiling at him.

"That old bastard is an expert in engineering and just about anything else," he thought as she flipped past him and entered the outer office.

"What are you going to do with her when you go back to New York on Sunday, Jed?" Carmen straddled the chair in front of Jed's desk, cocking an eyebrow quizzically.

"Carmen, m'boy, you never started it, so naturally, you wouldn't know how to finish it. But me, I'm adept at it. I've left 'em by the dozens scattered all over God's green acres. I just might decide to make it back here now and then for the weekend, and that will be the extent of it," Carmen said.

"I kept her on the string the longest of any of them – but God, she's really something. That red hair of hers is natural, you know. Next spring, I'll be on that project in Colorado," he added.

Jed shrugged his shoulders, not bothering to finish the sentence.

"I signed up today with Cannaro's outfit," Carmen said offhandedly. "It means two years as a second engineer on that project in Egypt, but I'll come back as a first-class engineer."

Jed didn't seem surprised at the news, and Carmen felt a little annoyed. The job was a big plum to any young engineer.

Finally, with a grin, Jed congratulated him.

"I recommended you for that job, Carmen. They wanted me as a consulting engineer, but I refused. I'm getting too old to traipse all over that Godforsaken place. But you, boy, can do it, and now is your big chance. You'll be rated higher than a first-class engineer when you get back."

"Thanks, Jed," Carmen said simply. "I might have known you were behind it. I'm starting back to New York tonight, but I'll probably see you there before I sail."

"Righto," Jed replied as Carmen moved towards the door. "Wait a minute, Carmen, and I'll ride down to the hotel with you. Everything is cleared away here. The B.W.S. has their maintenance staff all set up, and I've squared away, so we might as well have a drink before you leave."

"It's quiet in town today," Carmen remarked as he drove slowly through Gainesville.

"With the dam finished, it will be quieter yet by next spring," Jed answered. "It will take these people a long time to get used to living on small wages again. Most of the younger ones will be leaving the valley eventually. They're too used to big money and excitement to settle down in a quiet town again."

Honest Jed paused thoughtfully, then continued in a somewhat rueful tone. "For some people here, this dam project was a godsend. To others, it's been a disaster. Nonetheless, the town progressed in many ways. We, and the people who worked with us and for us, have left our stamp here. Good or evil, time will tell."

Carmen stopped the car in front of the hotel. Already, the place looked different. No one loitered on the front veranda, and the bar wasn't lined with men as usual. Carmen and Jed took stools at the bar.

"How does it seem not to be rushed?" Jed asked as Frank served them their drinks.

"Last week, it felt good," Frank answered, "but I guess I'll have to be looking for another job in a couple of weeks at this rate. Homer could handle it all by himself right now if he had to. Just about all the dam workers left last week. Business sure as hell took a drop these last few days."

"Homer stashed away enough these last five or six years to last him a lifetime," Jed reminded Frank.

"Probably he did," Frank asserted. "Some in this town did, and some didn't. I didn't, but I'm footloose and fancy-free, so I think I'll head for a livelier place next month."

"That's the way it goes," Jed returned philosophically. "By the way, Frank, I won't be here for dinner tonight. Will you tell Homer? I have some unfinished business to tend to. I'll see you in New York next week, Carmen." Jed hurried out.

As Carmen rose to leave, he caught a glimpse of Jed's red-headed secretary as she walked past the hotel.

Two weeks later, Carmen walked up the gangplank of the U.S.S. Nikita. He paused by the ship's rail, lifting his hand in adieu to those who had come to see him off. A hand clamped his shoulder, and he turned to see Gene Mollen smiling at him.

"What the hell are you doing aboard ship?" Carmen asked in surprise.

"I'm on the same job and going to the same place you are," Gene replied. He was flat broke, a little tipsy, and in between women. This time, though, he was going to show his old man, senator or not.

The town didn't come to a standstill with the exodus of the dam personnel and the outsiders who had worked on the dam. Its pace, however, was considerably slowed. Some of the workers prepared to seek out other higher-paying jobs after they had received their terminal paychecks.

Their standard of living had risen along with their wages. The few jobs now available in Gainesville and the rest of the valley paid meagerly in comparison to wages earned on the dam project. They saw no reason to drop back to jobs that paid barely enough to exist on, so they left.

As chilling winds began stripping autumn of its multicolored resplendent robes, Gainesville took on the appearance of a ghost town, waiting for winter to wrap it in white snow.

GHOSTS DON'T FADE UNTIL YOU FACE THEM

GRACE HILL WALKED down Main Street, pausing on the bridge. She looked up and down the brook it spanned. It had been widened and deepened. The water was murky, not crystal clear, and showed its littered bed at times, unlike how she remembered it. Suddenly, she was transported back to six years ago. A remembered echo of old Maggie's voice rang in her ears.

"Yer man must be real busy today, Miz Hill." An impelling force made her glance up at the rooms over the barbershop. It wasn't Maggie sitting there by the window or anyone calling out to her. Marge Holnes sat there in much the same way that Maggie had. Almost imperceptibly, haughtily, she nodded to Grace.

Without being intentionally rude, Grace turned and walked down the street, past the barren, empty shell of Jake's restaurant. Her heart throbbed painfully as she hurried on. The air was quite chilly. Shivering, she pulled her coat closer to her. She noted that, without interest, the new buildings had sprung up at the time she had been gone.

Few people were on the street and those who were evinced little interest in Grace's presence in town. Those who knew her smiled, spoke pleasantly, and went on about their business. "At least I'm not being martyred as the fallen woman," Grace thought, remembering Sadie Grimes.

Perhaps the town hypocrites no longer demanded "a pound of flesh" from the hapless ones, fearing eventually they might pay in like coin.

With a half-smile of satisfaction, she paused briefly in front of Jhan's, then opened the door and went in. She slipped unobtrusively into the booth nearest the door and glanced casually about. Jhan was tidying up behind the bar, talking now and then to the one male customer sitting there.

He greeted her pleasantly when he came over to take her order, pushed a nickel into the jukebox, and went back to the bar.

The man sitting there, making wet circles with his glass on the bar in front of him, said something to Jhan, rose from the stool, and went over to Grace's booth.

"I thought it was you," he said by way of greeting.

"Hello, Jess," Grace said quietly.

"Mind if I join you?" he asked, sitting down across from her.

"Of course not, Jess. I'm always glad to see you," Grace answered.

"Have a drink?"

"No, thanks. I'm having coffee and a sandwich."

"Honey, it's sure good to see you. Are you back to stay or just passing through?"

"It depends, Jess. Tell me something," she said impulsively. "Is Jake around?"

"Well," Jess said hesitantly, "I guess you must have heard he sold the restaurant and his home."

"Not until a couple of days ago," Grace admitted.

"Well, he did, Grace. It's been over four months ago. I tried to talk him out of it, but he seemed determined. Right after the deal was completed, he left town."

"Where did he go? You must know, Jess. You were his best friend."

"Well, now, Grace, Jake asked me not to say anything about where he went. He's been pretty upset this past year. In fact, he hasn't been himself since you left him. Oh, there have been women," Jess admitted to Grace's skeptical look.

"But, he never got too involved with any of them. I guess deep inside, he never recovered from your walking out on him. He wanted to make a new start when he left here. Under those circumstances, I don't think

I should say where he is. It's water over the dam, Grace. Why don't you leave him alone?"

"You're forgetting one thing, Jess," Grace pointed out quietly. "I had a reason for leaving Jake, and you know it better than anyone else. Old Maggie and the whores that hung out there knew him as well as I did. Maybe not as well in some respects," she corrected herself, "but at least oftener."

With an embarrassed face, Jess said, "Forget about Maggie. She's dead and gone."

"It doesn't matter anymore," Grace assured him. "Tell me," she said sardonically, "who's taking her place? I've been around enough, Jess, to know there will always be a Maggie in town. It wouldn't by any chance be Jenny Hilbur, would it?"

"Nope," Jess grinned, "she left town with one. Marge Holnes rented Maggie's old apartment. Everybody knows she boozed up what money she had and that she's still boozing it, but no one comes right out and says where she gets the money to do it. I'll tell you one thing, though: she isn't as fussy as you'd expect one of the Holneses to be."

Grace's face betrayed nothing of what she might be thinking. "Somehow, I feel sorry for her," she said.

"I don't see what for," Jess objected. "She must like it, or she wouldn't be doing it."

"Jess, you don't understand women very well. Actually, you don't even like them very well. You use them, and that's the extent of it. You act like your father used to. You think he was a real he-man because he beat your mother into doing everything he wanted her to do, even beating you until you got big enough to stand up to him," she said.

"You hated your mother because she didn't take your part, Jess, but she was afraid of him. Maybe you were too young to understand then, but you're not now. You shouldn't disrespect every woman because you didn't respect your mother. It wasn't really her fault. Your father wasn't a he-man; he was just a plain bully. I wonder now if Jake's attitude wasn't just a reflection of yours."

"I do feel sorry for Marge. She came from a so-called nice family, but she wasn't ever allowed to think for herself," she continued.

"Everyone in her family took it upon themselves to do it for her. She was in love with Les Soules, but her brother said he wasn't in Holnes's class, so she wasn't allowed to marry him, only because he came from a really poor family. I wonder if they're satisfied now! They helped put her where she is. You just don't know what a lonely woman can resort to."

Jess grinned imperturbably. "You're pretty when you're mad, Grace. How the hell did we get on this subject anyway? Let's get out of here, go down to Hennesey's, and have some fun. You know, Grace, I don't blame old Jake in a way for mooning over you. We could have some fun together, you and me."

"You don't even tempt me, Jess," Grace answered bluntly. "All I want from you is to tell me where Jake is."

"First, you tell me, Grace, where Gene Mollen is. You left town with him and were seen with him here and there for months after. Did he throw you over for some new stuff? Is that why you're after Jake again?"

"I don't give a damn what you or anyone else in this town thinks about me, Jess, but I broke off with Gene after I left here. I neither care where he is nor where he went. He didn't throw me over, as you put it. In fact, he wanted to marry me. Don't think it wasn't tempting. He was good for my wounded pride," she said.

"I didn't realize until it was almost too late that he'd never stop drinking. Though I never saw him really drunk, he was never completely sober, either. It seemed he always had to have just enough to bathe everything in moonglow for him,' Grace said.

"I couldn't take it, so I broke off with him. I know now I never really loved him. I did have an affair with him. I'll be honest about that. I think back on it all; it was just the thought of hitting back at Jake. I'm sorry about it, but that is the way it stands. Other than Gene, there has been no one else," she said.

Then she looked at him in the eyes. "Maybe Jake and I both had a lesson to learn, Jess. If so, we've both had a chance to learn it. I hope we can put it behind us and start over. He's the only man I've really loved, and I have reason to think he feels the same about me."

Grace looked imploringly at Jess. "Please tell me where I can find him," she said. "At least give us a chance to talk it over."

"Too bad you want to waste all that loving on old Jake, honey. I still say I could show you what some of the real stuff is like, but as long as you feel the way you do, I'll tell you. Jake started up a two-by-four roadside restaurant just before you reached the hospital on the outskirts of Binghamton. He runs it by himself. Want me to take you there?" he grinned.

"No thanks," Grace refused. "I'll catch the Shortline bus at East Branch. I'm sure I'll get there faster and less messed up," she added sweetly.

She picked up her purse and walked out.

"Didn't you make out?" Jhan asked as Jess came back to the bar. "I didn't want to, really," Jess returned. "I was just testing for my old friend's sake. I wouldn't have thrown it over my shoulder, though, if she'd said yes."

GRACE FINDS HERSELF, COMES FULL CIRCLE

S HE HEARD A crackle of paper as she stepped out of her uniform. Becky reached into the pocket and retrieved the two letters she had received that morning and only hastily read. "I wonder if she's changed much," Becky mused as she read Aldeen's letter.

"Ten years can do so much to a person. She writes as if they've been okay for her and Doc, though. I can't imagine her with three children, though. Two boys and now a girl named after me. Two more years, and they will be coming back to the States," she thought to herself.

'We're bringing my brother-in-law back with us,' Aldeen had written. 'You must meet him, Becky. He's something of a legend in India.'

'I can imagine,' Becky laughed ruefully to herself. 'All fire and brimstone. No, thanks, Aldeen,' she vowed silently. Just maybe I'll be already married by the time you come home, she thought wistfully, wondering what it would be like to share the warmth of love with someone as Aldeen had. Even with the troubled start of her marriage, Aldeen had managed happily through the years.

'We're poor, dirt poor,' Aldeen had scribbled in her letter, 'but honestly, Becky, you couldn't wish for a healthier, happier crew than we are. John and Keith are regular little natives, and little Becky mimics the chattering monkeys half the time. The other half is so prim that she reminds me of you. I'm glad we've named her Rebecca.'

'So am I,' Becky acknowledged silently, laying the letter aside, along with the one she had received from Sarah. Impulsively, she moved to the phone, lifted the receiver, and placed a call to Sarah Sutton.

"This is Becky," she announced in response to Sarah's hello. "I'd like to come up for a visit if you can put me up," she said without preamble.

"I simply can't believe it," Sarah replied in surprise. "You're coming back here after all this time. Of course, I have room for you," she hastened on. "Oh, Becky, I'm so happy. When will you arrive? Are you coming by bus, train, or what?"

"Just a minute," Becky interrupted laughingly. "I've got my own car, and I'm driving. I'll leave early tomorrow morning. Just keep the coffee pot going until I get there."

"You bet," Sarah assured her, and with a mutual 'bye now,' Becky cradled the receiver.

"That's one thing I like about small-town people," Becky thought. "I've only written to Sarah sporadically in the last five years, and then I invite myself for a visit on the spur of the moment. Sarah makes me feel like we'd planned it for months. I simply can't wait to see her and George." She busied herself around the apartment, packed her bags, and retired much earlier than usual.

"This is the first time in months that I've slept the whole night through," Becky mused the next morning as she rolled over in bed to still the insistent ringing of the alarm clock. "I feel like a frisky young colt."

Jumping out of bed, she tilted the blind. It was just breaking dawn. After she had showered and dressed, she carried her suitcases down to her car. Panting a little, she came back to her apartment, giving a last-minute inspection to be sure she had packed all her personal belongings.

Looking at her watch, she noted it was twenty past six. The janitor certainly must be up by now, and too bad if he isn't, she thought. Locking the door behind her, she descended the flight of stairs and knocked on his door.

"Here are the keys to the apartment, Mr. Wessel, and also a month's rent the landlord wanted in lieu of notice. If you'll just give me the receipt, I'll be on my way."

"You've been a nice tenant, Miss Hawk, and I'm sorry you're leaving, but lots of luck anyway."

Thanking him, Becky pushed the receipt into her purse. She went out to her red roadster.

"I wonder why anyone as prim and proper as I'm supposed to be selected a red car." The thought flitted across her mind and escaped an answer as she got in behind the wheel. Less than two hours later, she stopped at a little restaurant in Roscoe.

"Is the road passable over Cat Hollow?" she inquired when the waitress placed her coffee on the counter, adding, "I haven't been around here since they built the dam." When she saw the waitress, she looked a bit puzzled.

"Oh, goodness, yes," the waitress replied. "The county and state took that road over, and it's been widened and macadamized. In fact, it's better over the mountain than going around by East Branch. That is if you're going through Gainesville."

"That's where I'm going," Becky replied.

"That's the road to take then," the waitress smiled.

"At least there isn't much traffic over this road," Becky reflected, relaxing behind the wheel as she slowed the car to a crawl going down the mountain. "It's almost a mockery to call this Cat Hollow anymore. Heavens, it looks pretty civilized. I'll bet there isn't a bobcat for miles around here." Suddenly, she swerved the car violently to the left, stalling the motor. A huge buck leaped down through the woods after just clearing the front of the car.

"Whew," Becky exclaimed, shaking. "That was a near miss. Guess it isn't as civilized through here as I thought."

Gradually collecting herself, she started the car, driving slowly down the mountain to where the Cat Hollow Road terminated abruptly in the one running on the east side of the dam region. She caught her breath in amazement at the panoramic beauty.

It was as if a giant canvas had been painted. The dammed water lapped softly against the road's bank, its bluish-green sheen reflecting distorted shadows along its edges in wavering patterns.

Becky swung left at the turn, driving on, barely recognizing the region where farms once were but were now inundated, including the homestead where she had grown up. She pulled off the road and stopped at the point where a sign designated a parking area. She gazed pensively over the water.

"I never thought I could stand to see it," she thought as memories crowded upon her. "But now that I have, it brings me nothing but peace. I should have come back years ago. Part of me belongs here."

A gentle breeze blew across the dam, lifting tendrils of hair off her brow. It felt as smooth and caressing as a mother's hand. Almost reluctantly, she geared the car into action, proceeding down the road parallel to and past the dam. The vastness of it awed her. It was just ten minutes past nine when she stopped in the driveway beside Sarah's modest frame bungalow.

"I'm so happy you could come," Sarah greeted her amidst their tears and embraces. "You haven't changed a bit, only prettier."

"Well, the years and marriage have done wonders for you, Sarah," Becky complimented her. "I've never seen anyone so happy-looking in my life and as slim as a young willow," she added admiringly.

Sarah led the way into the house carrying two of Becky's suitcases while Becky followed, carrying the other two.

"Bring them in here," Sarah said, setting Becky's luggage down in a small but comfy bedroom. "Here's the clothes closet, and the bath is beyond that door. Now wash up if you feel a need to, and then come on to the kitchen. Coffee's all ready."

"Oh, Sarah, you're just what I've been needing," Becky smiled gratefully. "I'll be right out."

Later, lingering over coffee, the two chatted gaily.

"It just doesn't seem possible that you've been away going on thirteen years," Sarah remarked.

"Right now, it seems like I've never been away," Becky returned, "and really, Sarah, I don't want to go back to the city ever again to live or any place like it for that matter," Becky added. "I'm going to stay right in this town and make up for everything I've missed these past years."

"By the way, that reminds me," Sarah told her. "I hear the school here is going to have to hire a school nurse this fall. Miss Galin is leaving in June. She's getting married to one of the teachers. He's from around Binghamton, and they plan on going back there. Just maybe you could take her place if you're serious about staying here. This is still a small town, though, Becky," she warned.

"Everyone and everything about it is still small-town. We've recovered from the dam furor, and the town is much the same as when you left. You're used to the city. Above all, I don't want to discourage you, but it would certainly be dull and quiet in comparison."

"It wasn't the bright lights and glamour of the city that held me there," Becky explained earnestly. "Oh, I tried to believe that, but deep inside, I felt dissatisfied. I made a high salary, but after a while, that ceased to be important, too."

"Sarah, I've a need to come back here," Becky continued, subconsciously lapsing into the country vernacular. "I've a need to come back, and I've no doubt the people here have a need for me."

"I'm sure you'll find a job," Sarah replied. "There's a new cooperative hospital just outside of Walton. They only finished building it a year ago. With your degrees, you could get a job there whenever you wanted to. I hear the pay is low, though. But for goodness' sake, enjoy yourself for a while before you think of getting a job. I love having you here, and George is all for it too."

"How is he, Sarah? Heavens, we've been so busy talking about me that I forgot to ask."

"Oh, he's fine," Sarah answered. "He should come home for dinner in another hour. He's still working in the A&P store. In fact, he was just promoted to assistant manager."

Becky looked incredulous despite her efforts not to.

"Don't look so surprised," Sarah admonished. "George has really worked hard in the store. You know, Becky, he wasn't dumb by a long shot. I know we made fun of him in a way when we were in school, but the only reason he didn't pass his exams was that he didn't want to," she said.

"The very next semester after Miss Johnson resigned, he got his diploma. After we started going together, he told me all about the crush he had on her. I guess I was a little jealous at first, but if so, I got over it. I finally grew up, and so did he. He left the farm right after we married and went to work in the store. He's done so well that the manager has recommended that he be sent to school in Buffalo next year to study management. We're really very happy, Becky."

"I'm so glad, Sarah. You certainly act it. How come no babies, though?" Becky asked.

"God's will, I suppose," Sarah said cryptically. "Well, I've got to clear up here. Why don't you go sit on the porch and rest, Becky? Then, later this afternoon, we'll take a walk uptown."

"We'll both help and then we can both rest," Becky replied. "I'm not an invalid, you know."

They were chattering a mile a minute when George walked in. He greeted Becky affably, genuinely pleased to see her.

"Well, the shy, diffident boy grew up to be some hunk of a man," Becky reflected, noting that while his features were too irregular to be called handsome, he nonetheless had a rugged attractiveness that was most appealing. The lunch hour passed quickly and pleasantly.

"Are you sure you want to walk uptown?" Sarah asked as Becky dried the last dish.

"Of course," Becky replied. "Tomorrow, we'll ride all around the dam or wherever you suggest, but today, I want to walk. I want to get back the feeling of being a human being. Part and parcel of the whole lot of this town. Not just a relatively important cog in a big piece of machinery like I was in New York."

"Well, come on then," Sarah laughed. "If you want to be a country hick, we'll get you started."

"Is there a store here that sells jewelry or something in that line?" Becky asked as they walked up Main Street. "I want to buy a gift for a friend's little girl. I suppose I could have gotten one in the city, but I wanted her to have something that came from my hometown. She's my namesake," she added in a pleasant tone.

"There's a little gift shop up the street. They have quite an assortment," Sarah informed her, "and guess who owns it? Our dear, dear friend Polly Howe, or rather Polly Hadden now. She and her husband came back here a year ago," she said, bringing back that long-ago incident now turned into a dissatisfying marriage.

"They don't seem very happy. Jim doesn't trust her out of his sight, and with reason, from what I've heard. She flirts with anything with a pair of pants. He brought her back here and retired from the police force right after her mother died. She has two children. Guess that's about all she and Jim have in common anymore. She's still a snob. Thinks she's better than the common herd."

Becky looked amused at Sarah's tirade but offered no comment.

They wandered up the street. Becky admired the new buildings scattered along its length, occasionally meeting someone who remembered her.

"I know so few people here now," she said wonderingly to Sarah, "yet the town seems the same."

"It is," Sarah replied, "but there are some new faces, of course, and some of the people were just kids when you left here. But you'll get to know everybody in a couple of weeks," she assured Becky.

They came to the gift shop and entered. The woman who came forward to wait on them had her blonde hair done in an upsweep. Her plain black dress clung enticingly to her curvaceous body, contrasting sharply with her soft, milky skin. Devoid of makeup except for brilliant lipstick, she made a striking picture.

An old, familiar feeling of inferiority engulfed Becky as she recognized Polly Hadden. Like Sarah, she remembered the snubs and sneers that Polly had given them when they were in school together.

Almost instantly, she regained her poise, spoke pleasantly to Polly, and asked to see a baby's chain necklace. Polly's curiosity overcame her snobbiness as she greeted Becky. "She's certainly done all right for herself," she mentally noted, taking in Becky's smart tailored suit.

"Are you back visiting the sticks?" she asked, showing Becky a selection of tawdry necklaces.

"It would seem so," Becky replied noncommittally. "Do you have anything better than these?" Becky asked. "I'd like this to be really special."

"Well," Polly replied, "I do, as a matter of fact. I have a little cross set with a chipped diamond in the safe, but it is much more expensive than these. I don't have much demand for expensive things around here," she added contemptuously. She looked at Becky doubtfully.

"I'd like to see it, please," Becky said assertively. "It'll do," she said, examining the tiny cross pendant and taking the eighty-nine dollars from her purse. "Wrap it in gift wrapping, please."

Polly didn't like the cool, nonchalant Becky, she decided, but a sale is a sale, especially one with a nice price tag attached to it. She made out the sales slip and looked up at Becky.

"I started to write Becky Hawk on this," she laughed. "Anyone would know you would be married by now. I'm sorry, what is your married name, Becky?" she asked sweetly, glancing overtly at Becky's bare left hand.

"It's the same. I'm not married," Becky replied coolly, though her cheeks held a slight warmth.

The shop door banged loudly. Becky turned slightly as a half-grown boy entered.

"Jim, will you please stop making so much noise?" Polly asked reprovingly.

"Sorry, Mother," he apologized quietly and went on through the shop.

Becky smiled. "Yours?" she asked, turning to Polly.

"Who else's?" Polly said irritably.

"He's a handsome-looking boy," Becky said. "It must be nice to have a son his age. Time does fly, doesn't it?" she asked innocently. "Let me see, Polly, you've been married fourteen years now. He must be about twelve or thirteen years old."

The boy came back through the shop just in time to catch the last few words.

"If you're talking about me," he said indignantly, "I'm past fourteen. In fact, I'll be fifteen in February."

"Oh, hush, Jim," Polly reprimanded. "Go do your homework."

Her face was an angry red.

"Well, it's nice seeing you again, Polly. I'll undoubtedly see you often, as much as I think I'll be staying around here for a while." With this, Becky and Sarah left.

"Who's she, Mother?" Jim asked.

"Oh, some of the trash that used to live around here years ago," his mother answered. "She probably couldn't get a husband in New York, so she came back here as a last resort," she said viciously, still smarting from her and Becky's conversation.

Jim whistled. "Boy, she's a looker, though."

"Go do your schoolwork," Polly yelled at him.

"That's one friend you haven't got," Sarah remarked to Becky when they got outside. "I told you she's still snobbish and catty. I think you took her down a peg or two, though."

"Really, Sarah, she's undoubtedly trying to build up her own ego, which took a beating when she had to get married. The incidence of premarital births is high, but this town apparently made her feel that she was the only one to make that kind of mistake, so she tries to make everyone think she's better than they are. She acts snobbish and all that just because inside, she really feels inferior, whether she admits it or not," she said.

"Really, I shouldn't have said anything to her, but I guess I'm pretty human at that. Actually, she can't be blamed too much. I'm really ashamed of myself for that little hassle with her. None of us here knew too much about sex when we were growing up, and what we did know was shrouded in shame. Heavens, do you know my mother was ashamed to tell me she was pregnant? Of course, I guessed it after I went into training. Pa wasn't as afraid to tell me as she was, but he felt a little diffident about it, too."

She glanced at Sarah, who promptly averted her eyes and flushed furiously. "Don't tell me you don't know all about the birds and the bees," Becky laughed at her discomfort.

"It's not that," Sarah replied to Becky's bantering, "but George doesn't think it's proper to talk about things like that."

Becky looked at her speculatively. "Just maybe that's one of the reasons they don't have a child. He's too darn proper," she mused, "but at least he seems to have cured Sarah of using foul language."

"My gosh! It's after three," Sarah exclaimed, glancing at her watch. "We'll have time to walk past the new school, and then I've got to get home."

"Don't bother if you're in a hurry," Becky said. "My feet are killing me anyway." She looked ruefully at her feet. "Next time, I'll wear something besides high heels."

"Oh, come on," Sarah urged, turning down Maple Street. "The school is really the town's best feature. You must see it now."

"You'll walk me to death," Becky replied, "but if I must see the town's pride and joy, then I will."

"That's the new Catholic church," Sarah pointed to the small stone and concrete building next to the school. "It's small, but then when it was built, there weren't any Catholics here except those that were migrants. Now, the town has quite a few converts, and some people who have never gone to church before have joined it."

"Becky," she continued hesitantly, "George and I both belong to this church. Neither of us had actually joined any other church before. However, we sometimes went to the Missionary Alliance. That was the church strictly for the no-accounts, remember? Well, there is no distinction in this church. Rich and poor alike belong."

"Certainly, everyone has a right to his own beliefs, Sarah. And if you and George are happy belonging to the Catholic Church, I don't see why you shouldn't be Catholics," Becky replied.

"Our folks were dead set against it," Sarah elaborated, "but we felt they didn't have any right to say anything. They never went to church themselves and never made us go. You know that. So George and I did what we felt was right."

"I'll go to mass with you next Sunday," Becky offered. "I often went to New York. We had a chapel right in the hospital."

"You're more understanding than my own family," Sarah replied gratefully.

Father Lamb came out of the rectory and down the short walk. He paused a moment to chat with Sarah and murmur a pleased response to his introduction to Becky, inviting her to church anytime.

"What a peaceful, saint-like expression he has," Becky wondered aloud after he went on down the street.

"To tell the truth, I wanted you to see the church and hoped we'd see Father Lamb. That's why I insisted on you seeing the school, knowing we'd pass the church too. I wanted you to know I was Catholic, and I couldn't think of any other way to tell you."

"To the average intelligent person, it doesn't make any difference what another's religion is, Sarah. It's just plain bigotry and narrow-mindedness on his part if it does."

They paused in front of the school in the shade of a large maple tree. It was three-thirty. The first and second graders were dismissed and marched out of the building in orderly file until they reached the sidewalk, then scampered along helter-skelter in groups of three or four.

Becky saw Sarah reach out and pat a golden-haired tot on the head. "That's Sally Shields' little girl. Remember Sally O'Connor? She married Lynford Shields. I think she has the prettiest little girl in town."

Becky detected a note of wistfulness in Sarah's voice and wondered if her own yearning was as obvious.

"I'd love working in this school," Becky said impulsively. "I think I'll make some inquiries tomorrow about that expected vacancy. Maybe I'm not qualified for something like that." She looked doubtfully at Sarah.

"Pooh, Becky, you know perfectly well that you can meet the requirements," Sarah exclaimed.

"As far as having my B.S. degree, yes, but I've no experience whatsoever in social health."

"I believe you would have to see the county health department. We'll talk about it later. Right now, we'd better head for home."

The tangy spring days waxed slowly into summer. While the sun beat inexorably down on the valley, a soft breeze blew across from the mountains, making the weather ideal, especially to Becky, who had grown used to the hot, sticky weather in New York.

"I never felt so rested and yet so alive," she remarked to Dr. Miles as she swiped another arm with alcohol. "There, honey, don't take off the band-aid," she cautioned the little girl.

"This is the last one for today, Miss Hawk. I'm late starting office hours now. Let's see," he scanned the forms on his desk, "we've got the third and fourth grades tomorrow. That's thirty-three more vaccinations, and we're finished."

Dr. Miles sounded a trifle disgruntled. "Think I'll have a sandwich before I leave. Want to join me?" he invited.

"Well, as long as it's on the school budget, I may as well," Becky laughed as they made their way to the school cafeteria.

"You seem to like this type of nursing," Dr. Miles mentioned to Becky as they munched on their sandwiches. Becky looked reflective. "How come," he pursued, "after all the years and experience in New York? Haven't you found it dull these past two years?"

"Anything but, Doctor," Becky finally answered. "Life is never dull once you've found your niche. In fact, nursing in New York was not nearly as inspiring as it is here. I love the people and their kids. I'm not just an efficient piece of machinery here. I'm a human being and treated like one."

"By the way," Dr. Miles suddenly digressed, "there was someone asking about you the other day."

Becky looked curious.

"Yes?" she urged.

"It was at the surgeon's clinic in Bellevue. Dr. Shaktel, know him?"

"Yes," Becky admitted, somewhat flustered.

"He's a great man, Miss Hawk. He seemed to make a point of seeking me out and invited me to have lunch with him after he found out I was from Gainesville. Much too casually, he asked if I knew you, how you were, etc., and sent his regards."

Becky detected the old clinical look in his eyes as he watched her.

"Dr. Miles," she answered, forbidding a smile. "I knew Dr. Shaktel very well, but other than being a friend, he couldn't mean less to me."

"Nonetheless, if ever I've seen heartbreak mixed with hauteur, I saw it on Dr. Shaktel's face when he mentioned your name. Forgive me, Miss Hawk. Perhaps my diagnosis is wrong," Dr. Miles said apologetically.

Becky extended her left hand.

"Doctor, see this," she said, turning her hand so the small diamond caught the sunlight.

"Well! Seems like I'm not too observant," Dr. Miles laughed. "Congratulations! Who's the lucky man, if I may ask?"

"You observe enough," Becky replied tartly, "but it just so happens I didn't get this until last night, and the man saves lives too, though not in the same respect that we do. He's the new pastor of the Missionary Alliance, Rev. John Thornton."

A flicker of surprise washed over Dr. Miles's face. "Why, I thought he was leaving for some foreign mission this summer."

"He is," Becky retorted. "In Lalibela, Africa, or rather we are."

"You see, that's why he never married before. His work took him to uncivilized areas in different countries at different times, and he felt it would be unfair to a family, that is, up until he met me," she added coyly.

"Oh, I may as well tell you the rest of it before you start comparing me with Dr. Shaktel. It so happens that his brother is a doctor. He married a friend of mine who graduated from nursing school at the same time I did. They both went to India. He wanted to do research there," she explained.

"His brother was working in the missionary field there also. They came back to the U.S. a year ago, and John filled the vacancy in this church until he was reassigned. I met John for the first time when I went to visit my friend. It was sheer coincidence that we finally wound up in the same town together. Strange, too, that out of all the men I might have become interested in, he is the only one who has really meant anything to me. He's so down to earth."

"What about this town and its people that you so dearly loved?" Dr. Miles questioned sardonically. "Or are you no longer dedicated?" he added.

"My, what a discussion this turned out to be," Becky said.

"Really, Doctor, I'm sincere when I say I love this town and its people. Once, I hated it when I was a young girl. Small towns can be cruel in some ways, especially to an oversensitive adolescent, which I was. But a big city can be cruel, too. The policy of survival of the fittest is manifested in its cruelty. Everyone wants to get ahead. It's push and climb, slip and repeat. Actually, one becomes introverted. Ambition becomes a monstrous pulsating thing that gnaws away at one's vitals, leaving nothing but an aching void encompassed by a hard shell."

"Oh, I didn't analyze myself when I was there passing out the best of me in small parcels to the flotsam of humanity. I thought I was being the somebody my parents wanted me to be. Actually, I was feeding a soul-destroying ego."

"On an impulse, I put it behind me and came back here. The town has given me back my proper perspective, or rather, I gained it by separating the gold from the dross. My symbol of success is not my status as a nurse alone but the understanding of my fellow men and myself. First, I accepted the town; then they accepted me."

"I think I'll make John a good wife. We'll never have money, of course, but our life will be rich all the same."

"Rich in the respect that Dr. Shaktel will never know. Being able to make a fabulous amount of money and having the public adore him and his colleagues in awe of him is a cardinal virtue. He has everything I thought I wanted at one time, but he's everything I don't want, really. That's why I ran away from him and the city. There you have my life in a nutshell," Becky smilingly stated. "Does it satisfy you, Doctor?"

"I'm sorry for Dr. Shaktel," Dr. Miles said noncommittally, "but anyway, lots of luck in the impending marriage and do enjoy yourself with your little savages in Africa. There are enough of them right here in this school to satisfy me. See you tomorrow," he said, leaving the cafeteria.

With an air of tranquility about her, Becky rose and went back to the nurse's office.

BERTHA AND BILL: THEIR CONNECTION

Bill Seymour and Bertha "Van" Edwards North (1997)

Bertha "Van" Edwards North wrote this book more than 60 years ago. The manuscript was rejected by publishers at the time, dismissed in the mid-1960s as too tawdry. But today, its unvarnished truth resonates and is acceptable, even tame by today's standards. Its fiction reveals lives rarely spoken of—quiet, complex, and real—and their fates. My grandmother died 23 years before I started editing this unpublished work of hers. In many ways, this book is a bridge back to her voice. Both the beginning and the end, the first and the last.

She was born September 17, 1914, in Fish's Eddy, not far from the Downsville, N.Y., area where she spent her early years. Life was simple, often harsh—outhouses were more common than indoor plumbing, and misbehaving children were corrected with a quick switch from the nearest bush. From that rudimentary beginning, she developed the grit and endurance that would come to define her. She moved to Middletown, N.Y., in the early 1930s to become a nurse, eventually raising a family first with George D. Van Druff—who died in 1949—and later with Raymond C. North, who died in 1981.

"Van" was the name she carried from her first marriage, and it stayed with her long after George's passing. The name became her identity not only from her first marriage, but because it was woven into the fabric of a hardscrabble profession during a time when medicine was transforming. The authority of doctors still loomed like that of a pope: respected always, but often questioned behind closed doors.

My grandmother was part of that world. In that growing city of Middletown, about 70 miles north of Manhattan, she tended to patients from cradle to grave—on hospital floors, in nursing homes, and on private duty in the homes of the elderly. Her care was quiet and uncelebrated, but it was steady and fierce.

The nursing culture of her era was something akin to a battlefield—a place where nurses coined their own shorthand for survival and solidarity. The head nurse was the "ward sergeant." New graduates, idealistic and still hopeful, were called "white hats." Night-shift nurses earned the nickname "nightwalkers" for their stamina and ghost-like presence in the quiet hours. "Med wranglers" managed the endless routines of medication rounds—tedious and fraught with risk in those days. And when emergencies hit, the "strap crew" or "code runners" moved in— handling psychiatric outbursts or medical crises like frontline medics. Long-timers were called "lifers," not with derision, but respect. They had seen it all.

Beneath this militaristic lingo ran a deep vein of compassion, dark humor, and kinship. Nurses depended on each other. They shared cigarettes, secrets, and sighs after long shifts. They built bonds that, like scars, marked the battles they survived together. When I heard my grandmother swap stories with her nursing friends, there was loyalty, sharp edges, and human tenderness. The voices of her characters echo the same throughout this book, which is part memoir, part memory, and entirely hers.

I was the first grandchild, born in 1956, living with her while my parents' rocky marriage teetered back and forth. We bonded. She became the person in whom I had absolute, unquestioned, never-doubting trust. She was the bright star that illuminated a path to safety, security, and love. I know for sure that without her I would have drifted into an abyss of discontent. Instead, I modeled her intellectualism, her compassion, and sensitivity for the neglected, forgotten and unfortunate in society, her passion for writing, and her love of irony.

I should also mention she was my nurse at her home when I was a frightened very young child subject to sudden medical issues requiring operations. She was always there for me.

She encouraged my writing, journalism and public policy interests. I earned special points upon graduation from Harvard's Kennedy School of Government in 1985 with a revered place on her piano for my picture as the Dean handed me my master's degree. She was always supportive of my long-time service in government and also for becoming an adjunct professor of writing and communications at colleges and universities in Connecticut. These interests symbolize so much of what she valued in life.

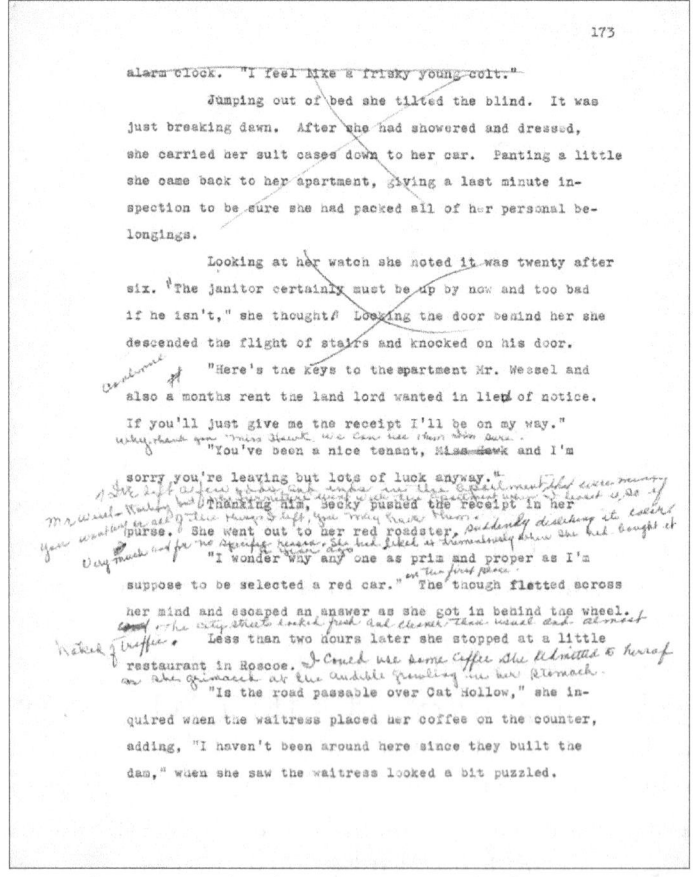

A page from my grandmother's manuscript in development, circa 1963.

There's much more to her legacy, but these touch points in my life bring me to help fulfill a dream never realized in her lifetime. This book's initial manuscript is indented from the typewriter keys used to form the words and sentences (and strewn with pencil erasures before white-out cleaned up that problem), and was hidden from light in a closed folder with additional handwritten pages. They could not remain in the darkness of my or anyone else's desk drawer any longer.

In what now may be my final and fiercest act of love for her—beyond living the values she taught me—I have fulfilled a promise: This book is now published. Sixty years ago, misguided literary agents dismissed her manuscript, blind to the bold, trend-setting genius it held. But I see it clearly now for what it is: a raw, revelatory testimony to a generation who refused the comfort of convention and dared to live on their own terms.

This book is her voice. You will see a time, day, and age—*Gone with the Wind*—reflected here in echoes of the tone and sentiment of that famous observation made by Rhett Butler at the end of the epic film with a core theme of a lost era. All I did was help her speak one last time—a goodbye long delayed in refusal to accept she's gone, an era that has passed and a quiet thank you for the countless times she gave me voice.

It is also her last gift to me - my first novel. In the twist of fate with an unpublished book, a manuscript never abandoned and prescience for a "beach read" skimpy on structure and high on drama, it's a true treasure in the changing fortunes of time.

She died on New Year's Day morning, 2000, as a century turned, though in my memory she remains forever in the previous one, the one most dear to her. She was 85 when her frail heart stopped. Yet, her heart still beats strong in all of us in the family today.

Bill Seymour
June 2025
Wakefield, R.I.

ABOUT BILL SEYMOUR

Bill Seymour is a journalist and writer based in Connecticut and Rhode Island. He is an adjunct professor at The University of Hartford and Manchester Community College. He organizes the Contemporary Issues in the Media series for Harvard University's John F. Kennedy School of Government New England Alumni Association. Bill also had a long career in public policy and political communications with the state government in Connecticut.

Acknowledgments

On behalf of the late Bertha "Van" Edwards North, she would want to thank her daughters, Linda and Cammie, for typing and retyping this manuscript through its early and numerous revisions. She would also thank the many people who contributed ideas for this book and their names passed with her when she died.

I. Michael Grossman of EBook Bakery in South Kingstown, R.I., has been a central force of encouragement and assistance in bringing to life my grandmother's long-shelved work. As a journalist, I interviewed Michael many times on his published works as well as those of other authors he helped to navigate the process of self-publishing.

My wish to publish this book has haunted me for more than 25 years after my grandmother died. Michael gave me reason, hope and belief that I could bring her voice alive in this book more than a half-century after she wrote it.

In addition, I would like to thank all the members of Rhode Island's South County Writers Group. Their bi-monthly meetings of critiquing each other's books in progress, essays and other written work sustained my perseverance to see this project through. The late Dr. Gene McKee, who wrote about his youth in *Caddie Days: At Point Judith Country Club* particularly inspired me as did Terry Schimmel and Yvette Baeu, both novelists. Other group members, Tom Brillat, Enid Flaherty, I. Michael Grossman, Kim A. Hanson, Gene Kincaid, Camilla Lee, Jane McCarthy, and Jill Moretti also provided insights from their own battles with the written word arising from their ideas, feelings and memories.

The book is enhanced thanks to some fact-checking by Town of Colchester, N.Y., Town Clerk Allison Gill and the compiled and publicly presented photos of the Pepacton Reservoir Dam at Downsville from the Historical Society's Facebook page and webpage, both overseen by Historian Kay Parisi-Hample.

Also, I found an invaluable understanding of the context of the Pepacton Reservoir Dam at Downsville in Lucy Sante's *Nineteen Reservoirs - On Their Creation and the Promise of Water for New York City*, with Tim Davis (for Photographs). Now in paperback, the book by Sante gives an "eye-opening tale of the greed and corruption, but also diplomacy and ingenuity" (*The Washington Post*) involved in the creation of the upstate reservoir system that makes New York City's existence possible—yet irreparably altered rural ecosystems and communities.

My newspaper editor, Paul Spetrini, at *The Independent* and *South County Life* magazine, has been wonderful helping to fashion prose into sterling sentences. Many of those lessons I brought to this book editing project. I also owe my writing mentor from years ago, Richard Galligan, more thanks than I can ever repay in multiple lifetimes for his commitment to teaching me to write in the mid-1970s. His lessons burn like a candle in the window and it never extinguishes.

I also would like to express my deepest thanks to the late Melody Currey, former commissioner in Connecticut state government and my close associate, who by happenstance, I learned came from Downsville. She and her mother read the manuscript over 13 years ago and confirmed its strong association with fact and fiction and all the juicy details in between!

In addition, I also want to thank Professors James Gentile of Manchester (CT) Community College, Joseph Manzella and the late Robin Marshall Glassman of Southern Connecticut State University, Jack Banks and Susan Grantham at the University of Hartford and journalist Yingjing Deng of the Harvard Kennedy School of Government New England Alumni Association, for their continued support in our shared interests in research, writing and unflinching quests in Proustian discovery of new eyes and the many universes they all see.

I also want to thank Cathy Elrick, Kathy Snyder and Susan Carocari for their influence on character development.

Any errors or deficiencies in this book are solely my own.

Bill Seymour

www.ingramcontent.com/pod-product-compliance
Lightning Source LLC
Chambersburg PA
CBHW072132170626
46813CB00004BA/1531